THE FORESTS OF DRU

SORCEROUS MOONS – BOOK 4

BY

JEFFE KENNEDY

AN ENEMY LAND

Once Princess Oria spun wicked daydreams from the legends of sorceresses kidnapped by the barbarian Destrye. Now, though she's come willingly, she finds herself in a mirror of the old tales: the king's foreign trophy of war, starved of magic, surrounded by snowy forest and hostile strangers. But this place has secrets, too—and Oria must learn them quickly if she is to survive.

A TREACHEROUS COURT

Instead of the refuge he sought, King Lonen finds his homeland desperate and angry, simmering with distrust of his wife. With open challenge to his rule, he knows he and Oria—the warrior wounded and weak, the sorceress wrung dry of power—must somehow make a display of might. And despite the desire that threatens to undo them both, he still cannot so much as brush her skin.

A FIGHT FOR THE FUTURE

With war looming and nowhere left to run, Lonen and Oria must use every intrigue and instinct they can devise: to plumb Dru's mysteries, to protect their people—and to hold fast to each other. Because they know better than any what terrifying trial awaits…

Acknowledgements

Thanks to Susan Conley, longtime family friend and knower of All Things Art, for coming out of Facebook lurkage to suggest that "retablo" was the word I was looking for. Yes, exactly – and it added so much to the story.

Hi there, dear, lovely reader!

So… You may have picked up THE FORESTS OF DRU thinking that it would be the last in the series.

(Hey—maybe it's the first book in the series that you're reading, in which case, it should work fine as a jump-in point. But, this explanation is for you, too.)

Long-time readers of mine know that I'm not very good at pre-plotting my books and series. Read "not very good" as "really can't do it at all." Stories tend to unwind organically for me. And often go on much longer than I think they will.

When I first conceived of the Sorcerous Moons books, I thought it would be a trilogy. I really did! Then the story deepened and became more complex than I expected. (You'd think I'd learn to expect this, as it seems to happen with all of my series.)

When everyone read book three, THE TIDES OF BÀRA, they quickly and cleverly discerned that Lonen and Oria's story didn't end there. I saw a fair amount of conversation online about how book four would end the series.

Not so much, it turns out!

But a lot of really interesting stuff happened in this book, so it should be totally worth it.

At this point, I'm thinking there will be six total. I'm pretty sure I can wind up the tale in two more books.

Thank you all for sticking with this series and spreading the word about it. This has been so much fun to do!

Thank you for reading!

<u>Credits</u>
Content Editor: Deborah Nemeth
Line and Copy Editor: Rebecca Cremonese
Back Cover Copy: Erin Nelson Parekh
Cover Design: Arel B. Grant, BZN Studio Designs

~ 1 ~

"WE WON THE war and this is still the best the king's table can command?"

Nolan poked at the meat with a sour scowl, and Arnon clapped him on the shoulder. "Not much of a homecoming, huh? You could have brought us game from the far forests and done better."

"I brought the King of the Destrye instead." Nolan shrugged him off. "That seemed more useful at the time."

Lonen, that selfsame King of the Destrye, didn't adjust his position to ease his aching side, lest his brother misinterpret that as a sign of discomfort with the topic of conversation. Nor did he miss the sidelong glance from Nolan that suggested he might be reconsidering Lonen's inherent usefulness. Not that Lonen could argue much otherwise. Being laid up in bed recuperating for more than a week didn't lend itself to high-profile—or even marginally effective—rule. Nevertheless, some remnant of his youthful self cringed, wishing he could do something to earn his older brother's approval rather than his scorn.

Mostly, though, he longed to be back in that bed, under the furs with Oria, sharing her warmth, basking in the surety that she slept beside him. To be there when the strange dreams woke her.

Oria hadn't wanted him to be up and about yet, but Nolan—believed lost in battle, now miraculously returned and restless with unsatisfied expectations—had decided he'd waited long enough for explanations. Rather than risk having Nolan barge into his bedchamber and interrogate Oria, Lonen had conceded to the lesser of the evils and gotten himself to this private dinner with his two remaining brothers. The last three of Archimago's line, sadly diminished in robustness of every kind.

But three was one more than they'd thought they had.

That had to be a good thing. A blessing from Arill herself. Somehow, though, under the sharp scrutiny of Nolan's piercing blue stare, Lonen nursed a few doubts.

He gave in and shifted, easing the pinch in his gut. The infection no longer poisoned him, but the massive tissue damage had yet to replace itself—however much ever would—despite Oria's foolhardy attempt to give her life to heal him. That side of his body sagged inward, as if part of him had been carved out.

Which, come to think of it, it pretty much had.

With a grimace for that, he forced himself to finish the slice of stringy roast on his plate, then picked up his warmed wine and drank, hoping to mute some of the ache.

"It's not good for you to be upright in a chair like this," Arnon said, frowning at him. "I can see it pains you."

"Father would say a warrior can suffer far more than a bit of pain, especially in the service of Dru," Nolan replied, gaze never wavering from Lonen. "He would have expected his successor to be sitting the throne and handling the pressing issues of the Destrye, not lying abed with a foreign mistress."

"You mean Her Highness, Oria, Queen of the Destrye?" Lonen didn't raise his voice, but his tone carried all the iron resolve of his battle-axe. Enough that Nolan sat back slightly, a hint of surprise flickering through his eyes before they sharpened again. *That's right. I am not the same little brother you knew before the war.* He might not be ruling impressively, but neither was he a pushover. Not anymore.

"She is Báran," Nolan said flatly, tempting Lonen to remark on his brother's powers of observation. But this was no time for levity. This conversation had been a long time coming and Nolan clearly intended to have it out now. So be it—and Arill hold him in her hand for this battle.

"I'm fully aware of that, Nolan, as I met her in Bára, where she is in fact, a princess and should be queen of her people by her own right."

"What exactly happened there?" Arnon put in, full of curiosity. "What?" He gave Nolan's frown a scowl of his own. "You're not the only one who's been sitting on questions while Lonen concentrated on *not dying*," he added pointedly. "You've dragged him out of bed for this, so we might as well get the whole story."

"I'm not interested in this Báran princess's *story*," Nolan snapped. "What I want is to break this foul spell she's employed to ensorcell our brother and king. We needed to get him away from her devious influence if we're to have a hope of that. *Stories* can wait."

"I am not ensorcelled."

"She's a witch, Lonen—you know this."

"A sorceress, actually." Surreptitiously, Lonen scanned the shadows near the ceiling. Sure enough, the emerald gleam of Chuffta's eyes shone back from a high perch, his iridescent white body stretched into a low profile along the upper curve of a ceiling beam. Oria had sent her Familiar to spy on the conversation, even though Lonen had asked her to keep her friend and guardian close. He didn't like her to be alone. Not after what had happened to her without his protection when they'd arrived in Dru.

"You call it a pine, I call it an evergreen," Nolan replied. "It's the same Arill-cursed tree."

Lonen regarded his brother calmly. One benefit of battling hordes of golems, running out of water in the desert, and countless other ways he'd nearly died horrifically—it had become abundantly clear to him that arguments over minor details like semantics paled significantly as anything to get excited about. He'd have thought Nolan would have learned that lesson, too, during his trials and journeys.

"Trees are sacred to Arill," Arnon put in, ever the pedant, "so it's not technically correct to call it an 'Arill-cursed' tree."

Nolan turned on Arnon with a snarl, proving that temperance had not been one of the lessons he'd learned. Ironic, as Nolan had been the dreamer and thinker before the Golem Wars. Whereas Lonen, solidly third in line for a throne he'd thought he'd never have to sit, had been the irresponsible, playful one their father had despaired of teaching discipline to. Perhaps tragedy and the horrors of war worked to change people. Fire tempered some weapons to greater strength and destroyed others.

"Queen Oria is a sorceress, yes," Lonen said before his brothers could come to blows. "She wields powerful magic, but she does so with heart and conscience." He eyed Chuffta in the shadows, certain her spy would be faithfully relaying the conversation, and chose his words carefully for both audiences. "Instead of staying in Bára as their queen, Her Highness married me and journeyed here at great risk to herself, sacrificing her own throne out of a sense of responsibility to the Destrye, in order to help us." And to keep a personal vow to him, but that should remain exactly that—personal. He held her promises to him close to his heart, treasuring them alongside her confession that she loved him. Precious gifts from a prickly and dangerous woman. They did not need to be scrutinized by others.

Particularly those who couldn't—or wouldn't—understand what lay between him and the foreign bride who'd brought a bright face to the terrible magics wreaked in the wars, and light into his own darkened heart. She might have made the difference in him becoming the tempered weapon, rather than the warped one.

Nolan sighed heavily. Pushing his plate aside and leaning elbows on the table, he laced his fingers together except for the index fingers, which he pointed at Lonen. "Your obvious sentiment aside, let's discuss the legality of this marriage."

"It's a legal marriage, Nolan."

He waved that off. "Only according to Báran law, which is not ours. We do not recognize it."

"I recognize it, and I was there." The onerous ritual had nearly knocked him unconscious and had left Oria in a dead faint. The magic connection hummed between them, Oria a warm flame inside him. The only time since their marriage that he hadn't felt it was when they'd been separated, both near death. Something he never intended to endure again— and something else he wouldn't attempt to explain. Before he'd experienced it for himself, he wouldn't have understood it either. Nolan opened his mouth and Lonen held up a hand. "A moot point anyway, as I intend to rectify any lingering legal qualms by marrying Oria in Arill's Temple, just as soon as we can both stand upright for the entire ceremony." *And dance afterwards,* he promised himself. Oria would see how a wedding—and wedding night—should be properly celebrated.

He flicked a glance at Chuffta, hoping Oria had gotten that particular message. She could be stubborn, but he'd have his way in this.

"Well, let's discuss that," Nolan said.

"No."

Nolan made an impatient sound. "I want you to hear me out on this."

"No."

"There is no need for you to marry her, Lonen! Keep her as a trophy of war, if you must. Our warriors have a history of that. It's somewhat outdated, but the tradition is an old and stirring one that celebrates Destrye victory. We can play it to the people that way and they'll see you as all the stronger and more vital for it. Don't ask them to accept a foreigner—the enemy!—as their queen. There's no reason to do so and it makes you look weak. Your people deserve a Destrye woman as their queen."

Lonen shrugged. "They won't get one."

"Can she even quicken with your seed? We have no way of knowing if Destrye can breed with her kind. She could leave you without heirs."

"There are Ion's sons, if so."

"It's one thing for that to be a last resort, another for you to go in knowing she won't give you heirs."

"What man knows such things for certain when he marries?"

"What about Natly?"

Lonen tightened his jaw. "She's irrelevant to this conversation."

"Hardly. She waited for you to return, believing the two of you to be engaged. She could still be your queen."

At Nolan's suggestion, Arnon dropped his face into his

hands. He and Lonen had spoken about Natly before, with Arnon arguing strongly against Natly as an appropriate queen.

"It seems to me," Lonen said slowly, measuring Nolan, "that you, yourself, rejected Natly as a suitable queen."

His elder brother had the grace to wince. "Yes, well. It need not be Natly, but—"

"It's a moot point. I've made vows and I intend to keep them. Would our people want a king who breaks his vows?"

"You mean like your betrothal to Natly?" Nolan shot back.

Lonen clenched his teeth against returning the bite. "I never promised. She assumed."

"Perhaps you are becoming the politician, parsing terms and dividing rope fibers."

"Perhaps so," Lonen returned, ignoring the sneer in Nolan's voice. The accusation was a fair one. "But I *am* king. I realize I shouldn't be. Arill knows our father died too young and this crown should be his." Lonen waved a hand at the wreath of hammered metal leaves he'd worn to the dinner. He didn't much care for it, and he'd worn it mainly as a reminder of his authority to his elder brother. At least it was light, even if he felt vaguely like an imposter wearing the thing. "Ion should have lived to succeed him, as we all believed he would. And yes, Nolan—you should have been king in his stead. Would have been, had we but known you lived."

Nolan's jaw flexed and he sat back, crossing his arms. "It wasn't as if I had a way to send a message. It took us weeks to find our way out of those caverns. If not for the underground lake that cushioned our fall, we would have died of thirst." He shook his head, a ghost of his old smile crossing his mouth behind the neat beard. "I tell you, it pissed me off mightily that I might die of *drowning* of all things."

"What did you do for food?" Lonen asked.

"You haven't gotten to hear this tale." Arnon poured them all more wine, clearly cheered by the turn in conversation. "It deserves to be set down as an epic ballad of its own."

"You tell it." Nolan took his cup, staring into it. "I'm weary of it, myself."

Arnon, who never met a topic that wearied him, grinned with enthusiasm. "So, there they were, Nolan and his regiment, on the north flank of the city. Fireballs hurtling through the air, golems everywhere, whirlwinds whipping through the center of the battlefield, while lightning forked overhead."

Lonen adjusted his position, sitting back to enjoy his brother's tale—and not bothering to point out that he'd been there, too. No sense interrupting the story's rhythm. He kept an eye on Nolan, however, darkly brooding over his wine.

"Then *crack!*" Arnon slapped his hands together, making both of his brothers jump and grinning at it, Arill take him. "The ground shook and opened up. Nolan and his men raced away from the edges, but no man can outrun the earth itself. The ground disappeared beneath their feet, and they fell, plummeting to certain death."

Nolan wiped a hand over his forehead and Lonen nearly called a halt to the story, but Nolan caught him looking and pierced him with a stare so challenging he knew it would only give insult. Instead he silently toasted his brother's bravery. After a slight hesitation, Nolan dipped his chin.

Oblivious to the exchange, Arnon continued. "Our hero, Prince Nolan, managed to grab a handhold and cling to it, as did a few other men. But the ground continued to shake, crumbling beneath their hands, while horses, supplies, even golems rained around them. They fell, too, sending a prayer to Arill to guide their steps to the Hall of Warriors."

"My prayer was nothing so coherent," Nolan interrupted.

"Shut up, this is my tale now," Arnon replied easily. He was doing this on purpose then. Telling the elaborate story to defuse tensions. Good on him. "But instead of waking in the Hall of Warriors, our hero plunged into icy water, cold and black as the sea. He drove for the surface, hampered by the rocks, men, horses, and supplies also teeming in the water."

"Grim," Lonen said, and Nolan raised his brows in acknowledgment of the observation. There. A bit of connection. Lonen would have to tell his brother the story of swimming through the bore tides of the Bay of Bára, carrying an unconscious Oria, nearly drowning all of them.

Or perhaps better not to.

"No light penetrated so deep in the earth," Arnon described with ghoulish glee, "but Arill held our hero in her hand, guiding him to swim to an unseeable shore."

"I mainly tried to swim *away* from flailing hooves and falling rocks," Nolan pointed out acerbically.

"Do *you* want to tell the story after all?" Arnon rounded on him.

"No, no—you go ahead. Never mind the fact checking."

"Thank you. Prince Nolan, chilled to the bone, exhausted and aching from the fall, at last dragged himself onto a dry shelf of stone. A few other men made it also, along with several horses—still with their packs, thank Arill."

"How many men?" Lonen asked out of habit before he caught himself. "Never mind, it—"

"About three dozen survived the fall," Nolan answered, gaze glittering. Out of a regiment of more than a thousand warriors. Horrifying indeed. Of course, they'd thought none had survived the chasm at all, so there was that. "Ten of those didn't survive the first few hours, and we lost three more on the journey to Dru. I brought fewer than two dozen home."

Lonen closed his eyes and sent a prayer to Arill to fete the lost soldiers well in the Hall of Warriors—and to forgive him that he felt some relief at the smaller number of bodies to feed and keep warm through the winter.

"You're jumping the story," Arnon accused.

"Apologies, brother." Nolan at least sounded less dour.

Arnon grunted, but continued. "Only three dozen men survived the fall," he intoned, "and ten of those didn't survive the first few hours."

Lonen passed a hand over his mouth to hide his smile.

"In the blackness of the caves, they might have been lost had Prince Nolan not been an educated man, as well as an experienced woodsman and hunter. Discovering that a phosphorescent fungus grew on the rocks, he reasoned that, like the moss on trees in the forests of Dru, it might grow more densely on the north face, and he navigated accordingly."

Lonen whistled, impressed, and Nolan refilled his goblet, shaking his head slightly, but not interrupting.

"As they continued, they discovered a well-worn passage. One that led more or less directly to Dru, and in fact emerged into a dry lake bed somewhat north of us." Arnon waited, expression expectant.

The wine evaporated on his tongue and Lonen found himself sitting upright, the pain in his side a minor consideration. "Wait—an underground passage from Bára to Dru?"

Nolan gave him a long look. "At least to the region north of Dru, but it appears so."

"That's how their golems traveled here. And how they drained the lakes so quickly before we became aware, sending the water back to Bára."

"The passage might have acted like an aqueduct, an underground river carrying water from our lakes to theirs until it had drained completely. They might have made others over however many years, with many routes to the surface, which would explain how the golems managed to pop up so unexpectedly and disappear again," Arnon agreed.

"Why didn't you tell me about this before?" Lonen demanded. So many possibilities. How could they use this to their advantage? Of course, they'd thought the golems had been eliminated following the fall of Bára and that their major problem now lay in incursions by the even more deadly Trom, who needed no underground passages, instead flying in on their enormous dragons that scorched crops and Destrye alike. But he had nearly died under the fangs and claws of a band of golems he and Oria had encountered on their journey. "If we could—"

"*Why didn't we tell you?*" Nolan interrupted in a tone as scathing as dragon fire. "There was the small problem of an enemy princess in your bed. She of the people who sent the cursed goblins. We could hardly discuss such sensitive matters in her hearing. Arill only knows what her plans are or what information she'd send back to—"

"Oria is a not a spy." Lonen set his teeth against saying more. Steeled himself not to look up at her actual spy, concealed in the beams above.

"How do you know that?" Nolan demanded, angry and bewildered. "*Think,* man! You acknowledge she's a powerful sorceress. She could easily work magics to cloud your mind. She could be here to finally and completely undermine Dru. What better way than to capture the attention—and, incredibly enough, the hand in marriage—of our king? How is it possible this has *not* occurred to you?"

"Because I know her," he snapped. And he knew the many reasons she'd fought against him bringing her to Dru. Ones not at all politic to divulge. "I know what goes on in her heart and mind."

Nolan threw up his hands. "No man knows what goes on in the heart and mind of a woman, and that's if she's Destrye and not a foul Báran sorceress."

"Be mindful how you speak of your queen."

"I have pledged that woman no fealty."

"You will," Lonen replied evenly, putting the weight of command behind it. "Or do you mean to challenge me as king?"

"And bring civil war to Dru, on top of everything else? Oh, that's a grand idea."

"Are you asking me to abdicate in your favor?"

Nolan's face was perfectly neutral, an impenetrable mask. "Are you offering?"

"It's been suggested that I should abdicate in favor of Ion's son, Mago. His claim takes precedence, even over yours."

"That was before the Trom attacked," Arnon cautioned. "We discussed it as a peacetime proposition because we believed the war had ended—and because Salaya campaigned for it. I never thought it was a good idea, even if it might ease her widow's grief, and would not support that measure now. We are as much at war as ever and Mago is too young to bear such a heavy responsibility. In times of war, a warrior must lead."

"I am a warrior, and not too young." Nolan gave them both long and pointed stares. If all had gone as it should, he would have been crowned king. It never should have been Lonen and they all knew it.

"By Destrye law, I became king the moment my father and older brothers died," Lonen spoke slowly, feeling the weight of it himself. "I believed you dead and grieved your loss, brother, with never a thought that you might have survived." Not exactly true, but the haunting terror that his brother might be trapped beneath the earth, broken, bleeding, and slowly dying without succor wasn't worth plaguing them with. "I took the sword of the Destrye from my father's dead hand. A hand that had been turned to jellied flesh by a monster so heinous it dropped my father and his heir with a touch, reducing every bone in their bodies to pulp. I had to wipe the hilt clean of unnameable substances just to keep my grip."

He paused to gather himself, his brothers watching with ill-disguised horror.

"I didn't want it, never sought to be king, but I took that responsibility," Lonen told Nolan. "I assumed the weight of it over their dead bodies, as my heritage demanded I do, and I negotiated our truce with the Bárans." He put down the wine goblet with a thump when Nolan opened his mouth. "It doesn't matter that the truce was violated by *some* of their people. I did my best by the Destrye, as our father would have wanted. We came home to a decimated people, but I kept going. It was on me to find a way to save us and by Arill, I have tried."

"You've done more than most men could have," Arnon said. "The aqueducts. Planting the late crops. Rationing food and water. Planning for winter. Nolan, he nearly killed himself, and this after a long and exhausting campaign."

"I don't question any of that," Nolan replied.

"But you question my competency now."

"I think you should consider that you might be compromised."

Silence fell among them, sharp-spined and treacherous to navigate.

"And you, Arnon—what do you think?" Lonen asked his

younger brother.

"We don't know her," Arnon said quietly. "You ran off to Bára to demand answers, to hold this princess to her vow that they would observe the peace and no longer attack us, steal our water, burn our crops. I looked at that sword every cursed day and made myself consider that you would likely never return for it. Every time I made a decision in your name, I dreaded the day we'd reconcile ourselves to your death, and I'd have to hold the throne for Mago. If the Destrye survived long enough to for him to grow up.

"And then you returned—more than half-dead and apparently married to this Báran sorceress—who for all we know sent those attacks, who has swayed your heart and mind to the point that you snarl at us for asking the simplest of questions. We try to give you space to recover without her influence, and you barge into the ward for Arill's Blessings—the women's ward, even, where men are expressly forbidden to enter—you terrify our head healer, roar orders in all directions, install the sorceress in your bed, and refuse to admit anyone but a few servants. If not for them we'd wonder if the sorceress yet lived. You won't even admit our healers to tend you, though you need it badly."

"That was you who ordered Oria sent to that charity ward, who kept her from me?" Lonen gripped the arms of his chair, rather than strangle Arnon.

"We decided together," Nolan said, jaw tight.

"You had no right to—"

"This is the first time since you've returned that we've been able to talk to you." Arnon thumped a fist on the table in a rare show of frustrated temper. "What in Arill do you expect of us, Lonen?"

"I expect you to believe in and support me. If not because

I'm your brother, then because I am your rightful king, whether any of us are happy about that situation or not."

"It's not that, Lonen, dammit." Arnon raked his hands through his already messy brown curls. "If it were one of us, you would do the same. If you believed we'd been captured and controlled by a sorcerer—and up until recently, you agreed their magic was an abomination against Arill, too— then you would fight to help us also."

"And I'm telling you that I am not controlled and I don't need your help. Oria is here to help *us*, to protect us from the Trom. You'll see."

"See what?" Nolan spread his hands wide. "They're gone and the damage has been done. You lost most of the unharvested crops. We have no nearby fresh water supplies for all these people hunkered down for the winter under the wings of Arill's Temple. You've made little progress in shoring up what was supposed to be emergency construction and not long-term housing. And there's no indication these 'Trom' and their 'dragons' will return. We have nothing left worth taking."

"Any number of people can bear witness to what the Trom and their dragons did," Lonen said. "Don't try to make it sound like a child's tale."

"My point is that we have bigger problems than you dreaming up some implausible cause for your sorceress wife. If I were king, I—"

"But you're not." Lonen cut him off and Nolan's piercing gaze flashed with anger before he directed it ferociously at his wine. Lonen choked back the temper and sighed. "We're all stuck with me being king, like it or not."

"There is legal precedent," Nolan said, not looking up, but staring into his cup, "for a king to be deposed by another with an equivalent or more potent claim to the throne."

"That civil war you mentioned?" Lonen tried to keep it light, but the implicit betrayal stung.

Nolan flicked a sharp glance at him. "Nothing so large scale or destructive. A duel would allow Arill to select her champion, according to the old ways."

Arnon drew a sharp breath. "Lonen is barely out of his sickbed. He cannot duel with you, even if Arill's priestesses agree to such an archaic ritual."

"If you wanted me murdered, brother," Lonen replied, holding Nolan's gaze, "you would have done better to leave me at the spring. I could have died in peace and you would not have had to sully your hands with my blood."

"I've thought back to that day." Nolan's eyes were dark. "And sometimes regretted my part in it. Particularly that I brought that viper of a sorceress here instead of leaving her there to fertilize the forest as I should have."

"I would have killed you for abandoning her."

"A dying man held no threat to me."

"I'm not dying now."

"And you may yet get the opportunity to try to kill me," Nolan replied, with no apparent emotion.

"Brothers—" Arnon began.

"I've had enough." Lonen cut him off. He drained his mug and eased to his feet, no longer bothering to hide the wince of pain. "Such a heartening interlude this has been. So worth leaving my sickbed for."

"Go back to her then," Nolan called after him. "She is pretty enough to distract you for a while. But you have to get out of bed sometime."

"Lonen." Arnon caught up to him, expression earnest, eyes grave. "Let the healers tend you. Give us that much."

"Not Talya," he growled. If he saw the woman, he might

strangle her.

Arnon held up his hands. "Fine. Not Talya. Who?"

A fine question. "Baeltya."

"Isn't she a junior healer?"

"Yes. And she tended me when I was but a junior prince. She has a good manner." A quiet one that might not disturb Oria too greatly. "Send her."

"I will." Arnon gripped his shoulder. "We're on your side, brother."

"Then show it." He shrugged out of Arnon's grasp and strode away.

Alby, Lonen's lieutenant, met him outside the doors. He made no comment, but stayed closer than usual. Perhaps he thought he needed to be ready to catch Lonen if he fell, which meant he must look nearly as bad as he felt. Lonen would not let himself fall, however. They walked slowly down the long hall, as Chuffta slipped in through a crack in the ceiling and winged his silent way ahead of them.

~ 2 ~

"*H*E'S LEFT THE *dining hall and is coming your way,*" Chuffta spoke into her mind. *"He's not happy."*

Oria restrained a sarcastic reply. As wise and clever as her derkesthai Familiar could be, the intricacies of human interactions sometimes escaped him. He'd faithfully relayed Lonen's conversation—if you could call it that—with his brothers, but that didn't mean he'd understood the nuances of all that had been said. So, instead of snapping at him, she vented her righteous anger by pacing in front of the stone fireplace. The room wasn't as big as her old rooftop terrace, but it gave her a decent amount of space to work out her annoyance. Especially since she had only her own emotional energy to wrestle.

One upside of having figured out how to shut out the cha-otically overwhelming input of the wild magic: she didn't run the risk of overload of that variety. Small compensation as that also meant she had no way to replenish her magic, either. Nothing to be done about that.

She didn't blame Lonen's brothers for being suspicious of her—in fact, she'd warned Lonen countless times that his people wouldn't welcome her with open arms. She loved the Destrye warrior immensely, probably unwisely, definitely without meaning to—and that included his propensity for irrepressible optimism—but for once he should have been able to predict this inevitable outcome.

Things didn't turn out rosily just because he was so sure they would.

No, of course his brothers had questions—but the way they'd sneak-attacked Lonen had her burning with fury. She'd met them both only glancingly. *We don't know her.* Arnon's words echoed with quiet menace in her head. Along with the others they'd used. *Sorceress. Foul. Viper.* They didn't know her, but they distrusted, even hated her. Fine. That was to be expected as their people had been enemies for so long.

How could they show so little faith in Lonen, though? The Destrye warrior was everything that was noble, honest, and stalwart.

The doors to the outer chamber opened and after a moment, Alby stuck his head in to check the bedchamber, gave her a nod, and then stepped back for his king to enter. The lieutenant at least always treated her with neutral deference. He closed the door, leaving them alone. Lonen moved stiffly, with more than physical pain. Composing herself—restraining the impulse to go help, which would only get her snarled at—she arranged the supporting pillows in his favorite armchair near the fire and picked up a wine carafe.

"No more wine, love," he said, dragging the wreath of hammered metal leaves from his hair and tossing it on a chest, then unclasping his indoor furred cloak and throwing it on top. He made his way to the chair and eased himself into it. "My mind is foggy enough. I've apparently lost my head for drink these last weeks."

"Not surprising, as you've fallen out of training for it."

He snorted, the fresh scar over his right eye creasing as he stared into the fire where it leapt behind the intricately designed metal screen. Chuffta arrived from somewhere and settled himself into his favored nest on the hearth. The servants had quickly gotten over their fear of the winged lizard and had taken to spoiling him outrageously, with Alby setting the lead, bringing him all sorts of meaty nibbles and soft furs sized just for him. They assumed he was a pet, more like a favored hunting hound, and Lonen and Oria had decided it was best to let them continue to think so.

"Are you comfortable? There are more pillows."

"Don't fuss."

Aha. Those barbs aimed at his warrior toughness had lodged under his skin. Fine then. "How was the meeting with your brothers?" She tried to sound idly inquiring, fiddling with her own goblet of well-watered wine. She greatly missed her favorite fruit juice, but it was never among the food and drink served them and she wouldn't ask, lest Lonen feel guilt over something else he couldn't provide her. They might not have any fruit at all in this frozen realm.

No guilt in him now, he eyed her with some acerbity. "You're going to pretend Chuffta didn't relay every word?"

Ah, the guilt was hers, staining her cheeks with warmth. *"You were supposed to stay hidden."*

"I tried. There are not many places to hide in these enclosed rooms of theirs—and Lonen deliberately looked for me. No one else knew I was there."

Lonen was watching her still, knowing in his uncanny way that she conversed mentally with her Familiar. "I asked you to keep him with you."

"Clearly you suspected I'd disobey, as Chuffta says you searched him out," she replied stiffly.

Lonen massaged the scar. It had healed cleanly, but the way it crossed the path of that other, older scar made the skin around his eye pull. He'd developed a habit of rubbing at it when distracted or in thought. "I *requested* it of you because I don't want you unguarded."

She shrugged that off, tucking her hands in her sleeves. They were always cold in this wintery place. It might also be a sign of her slow failing without a source of purified sgath. Something else she couldn't change. "You know perfectly well he doesn't always listen—and he's found all sorts of ways in and out of your wooden rooms and passageways."

"Oria," Lonen said in that patient tone that mean he didn't buy her explanation. "Can we dispense with this? I've had enough verbal fencing for the time being."

"Yes," she replied, chagrined. Thoughtless of her. "I'm sorry."

He slanted her a crooked smile. "There's your one apology for the day. Will you sit or are you determined to pace about like Buttercup stuck in a short stall?"

She huffed a breath at being compared to the massive black warhorse. "I'll sit, if we can discuss what your brothers said to you."

"Deal. Bring your brush and pull the stool over."

"My hair doesn't need brushing." What it needed—quite desperately—was washing.

"It soothes us both."

Which was true, so she fetched the odd brush he'd arranged for her to have. With a handle and back made of wood, carved into delicate, intricate vines, it fit nicely in the hand. The business end, however, was made from some kind of animal bristles. It seemed fur shouldn't be so stiff, but these forest pigs Lonen described apparently sported such stuff. Strange as it was, her hair liked it well, and it pulled at the tangles far less than the one she'd left in Bára when they fled.

Along with everything but the clothes she'd worn, all now consigned to the rag pile.

She tried to think of herself as unencumbered, gifted with a clean slate, rather than dependent on Lonen for every little thing.

Handing him the brush, she sat on the low cushioned stool between his knees, staring into the fire. He undid the knot she'd put it in, then the tie that held her braid and unraveled that. "I think you should leave your hair down," he commented, not for the first time.

"It gets in my way," she replied. Maybe he didn't notice that it needed washing. Hoping so, she refrained from saying anything about it, lest she lessen his pleasure or dull the moment.

Gathering the long fall of her hair, he ran the brush through, making a wordless hum of pleasure. Because of her particular limitations, they couldn't touch physically—not skin to skin—so his solution of indulging himself in touching her hair served as a substitute, however poor. It did relax her, however, and seemed to make him happy. As much as a sexless marriage could. His brothers just had to bring up Natly, Lonen's former lover. Oria had yet to see the Destrye woman in the flesh, though she'd glimpsed her in Lonen's mind.

A bitter irony, though, that Nolan had asssumed Lonen couldn't pry himself out of bed for luxuriating in sex with her, when they'd never had actual intercourse at all. One of a number of things about her Lonen had not divulged.

"I notice you let them believe I have my full powers," she finally said, since he didn't seem to be planning to speak first.

He remained silent a bit more. "It's better if they fear reprisals from you. And I'm confident you will yet regain your magic."

"Does nothing dim your optimism?"

"It's not optimism," he replied with hushed ferocity. "It's necessity. You're too thin, too pale. We need to find magic for you, and soon."

His intensity took her aback. "Well, I don't know where I'd get it from. I can barely touch the wild magic before it knocks me unconscious." And left her burnt to the core. Like trying to light a candle and having a bonfire blow up in her face.

"I have some ideas. Now that we're better, we can explore them."

"I'm fine. You were winded simply walking down to the dining hall."

"You're not fine," he said quietly. "You grow more wan by the day. Do you think I can't see it?"

She had hoped.

"Finding you a sustaining source of sgath is critical," he continued.

"Preparing for the inevitable incursions of more golems and Trom is critical," she retorted. "You and I both know Nolan is wrong—they'll return, and soon. Now that he's King of Bàra, with almost unlimited power, Yar won't waste the opportunity."

"Do you think he knows about those tunnels?"

The brush whispered through her hair as she thought, grateful that he allowed the change in conversation topics. Such an extraordinary revelation, the tunnels. "I really don't know. I didn't know about them—or that lake—but my father, even my mother, kept their secrets well. There was a great deal I didn't know before the siege. It's difficult to say what they might have shared with my brothers. With Yar the youngest and always..." Not easy to pick a single word to encompass Yar's character flaws. Understanding her pause, having helped her battle her younger brother for the crown, Lonen patted her hip, giving her tacit permission to move past it, too. "Anyway," she sighed, "I can't see that they would have shared information that sensitive with him. And if they knew we had a lake beneath Bára, why steal water from Dru?"

"That occurred to me, too."

"Perhaps it was a secret among few that was lost," Chuffta put in.

"True. Chuffta points out, rightly so, that the tunnels might have been built long ago to carry the water from your lakes to Bára, and even her sister-cities. The lake might not even have been for storing the water itself, originally."

"What do you mean?"

There had been a time she would have hesitated—no, absolutely refused—to share temple secrets with the Destrye. Moot now, along with so much else of her previous life. "You know how I explained that the coherent source of sgath lies below Bára, and that all her sister-cities have something equivalent?"

"Though each city is slightly different, which was why Gallia couldn't access Báran sgath as well as you could."

"Not right away, anyway." Hopefully Yar's beleaguered new bride had found a way to do so. She had enough trials stacked against her as it was. "But yes, each city is different—so I was taught, and Gallia's experience bears that out—though I don't know why that would be. It never occurred to me to wonder how the sgath got there. It always just *was*." So much she'd never examined closely enough, determined as she'd been to gain *hwil* and receive her mask as a priestess. Those goals seemed superficial and … juvenile now. "The priestesses replenished it, but that was a slow trickle compared to the enormity of the sgath stored."

"You think it has something to do with the lake?" Lonen broke into her thoughts.

"Maybe? Sgath is often correlated with water—it accumulates like a pool filling, it's dark, ever yielding, passive."

"Female."

"Yes." She laughed a little at that. They'd both learned that wasn't necessarily true.

"And grien, the male magic, is more like fire—active, forceful, bright."

"So the metaphor goes, yes."

"Then there's you, who somehow ended up with the ability to wield both."

"Against all reason and precedent."

"*As far as we know and you were told,*" Chuffta said. He appeared to be asleep, rounded white belly up before the fire, wings half splayed and rear talons curled in contentment, but his mind-voice remained animated and alert. "*I still think there wouldn't be such a strong prohibition against a woman wielding grien if it weren't possible. Has it occurred to you that there's no law against a man using sgath?*"

"*Because they can't—*" she began, then stopped herself. Or could they?

"*Exactly.*"

"Of course," she said aloud, to return to the point, "neither sgath nor grien are actual physical forces, so all of these descriptions are only analogies."

"But they exist in the world and affect physical things, so they must be physical."

She contemplated that. "I didn't realize you were such a philosopher."

"I'm not. Really we should put this to Arnon. He's the one who understands physics and such. He's the one who got us across the Bay of Bára by charting the bore tides and the influence of the moons' phases on them. Since you associate sgath with Sgatha and grien with Grienon, maybe he'll have ideas on how the moons affect the magic flows, too."

"You've been thinking about this."

"Long hours abed lend themselves to contemplation, even for those of us not much inclined to philosophy." He sounded drily humorous. A welcome sound. He'd once had an irrepressible sense of humor, even at the worst of moments. His extended convalescence had managed to drain him of that as nothing else had. Convalescence and worry for her.

"I'm thinking Arnon will not be inclined to discuss how to replenish the magic that frightens the Destrye so badly."

Lonen's turn to be quiet, sifting her hair through his fingers. "He'll come around," he said finally. "Nolan's been at him, that's all."

She bit her lip on asking, then gave voice to her most salient fear. "Will Nolan truly challenge you to a duel for the throne?"

Lonen grunted noncommittally.

"A real answer, please."

"Only Arill knows. It would be extraordinary, but we live in extraordinary times."

"Is it a duel to the death?" she asked quietly, as if saying it softly would give the words less power to evoke the reality.

"One can't have defeated kings hanging about to rally the disaffected."

"So that's a yes."

"The whole duel is theoretical."

"But possible—even likely," she insisted.

"A fine turnabout that would be for us, yes? First your duel for the throne of Bára, then mine for Dru."

"Hopefully yours would turn out better than mine," she muttered.

"Hey." He set the brush aside and coaxed her to turn to face him, touching her only over the thick fur robe she wore. It both kept her warm and cushioned her from casual contact. Lonen settled his hands on her hips. "You won your duel in spectacular fashion. You defeated Yar handily—it's not your fault the temple intervened and called your use of grien anathema. You're a sorceress of rare and amazing ability. I haven't forgotten it and neither should you."

"*Was* a sorceress, of unreliable, untrained, and unpredictable ability," she corrected. "I appreciate the support, Lonen, and I won't pretend that when you say such things, it doesn't turn my head, but you can't—"

"Oh yes? Tell me how I turn your head," he murmured, his mood shifting into languid desire, as he tangled his fingers in the hair falling over her shoulder, and leaned in to breathe against her cheek. "If it's anything like how you affect me, it must be dizzying indeed."

"It is." Well and truly dizzying, exacerbated by being so close to him. With her portals so tightly closed, she didn't feel his thoughts and emotions nearly as easily, not unless he projected strongly or they were very close. Skin to skin opened up all the channels from another person into her—to an unbearable degree that strained her to the point of collapse and coma if sustained too long, almost like contact with wild magic—but skin a whisper apart from hers sent the feel of him into her on a manageable level, much as his warm and spicy scent filled her head.

The anger his brothers had stirred up brooded dark in the background, but above that swirled a potent mix of affection, admiration, and pure lust. His masculine exuberance had drawn her to him from the beginning, even back then, when it overwhelmed her ability to vent the energy again. With his slow return to health, each day immersed her in more of the vital wash of his presence. Though she welcomed that as a sign of his recovery, it also made it more and more difficult for her to contain her own longing for him.

"Lonen…"

"Yes, love?"

"Stop." She tried to pull back but his hand wrapped in her hair anchored here there. "We can't do this."

He lifted his head, studying her face. "Because you don't feel up to it?"

"No, that's not it." That was the thing. She really did feel more or less fine. Kind of out-of-body sometimes, but not terrible. *Wan.* That described it well. "We just can't—"

"We're doing it," he murmured. "So it must be that we can. You're so lovely in the firelight, Oria. The flames make your hair shine like a copper drum hit by the golden light of sunset. You look good in my furs, too. Perhaps you have ensorcelled me, as the least glimpse of you makes me want to chuck all of this nonsense and run back to the oasis. Maybe I should never have made us leave."

The memory of that peaceful place—and the magical buffer that had allowed them to touch—made her ache with nostalgia, and more. If only she hadn't been too ill from the wild magic for them to truly be together. "Don't joke about that—it's not at all funny."

"That's the thing. I don't think I'm joking. The need for you burns in me stronger than anything else. Make love with me, sorceress."

She laughed breathlessly. "You're impossible. We can't do any more than this."

"This much is good, but we can do more. Remember?" He lifted the hair he held and kissed it stroking the locks along his cheek above his neat beard. "This is me, kissing you, caressing your skin, making you tremble."

She did tremble, going as hot and wet as when he'd said such words to her when they consummated their marriage. *I would be kissing you now. I'd start with light ones, like butterfly wings on your lips, lulling you in until you felt safe enough to open your mouth … Your lips wet and plump and pink from meeting mine … By now you'd have opened your mouth to me. My tongue would be inside you, tangling with yours.* The memory he deliberately evoked shredded her recalcitrance. "Lonen…"

"Ah, I love it when you say my name that way," he murmured, sliding the other hand that had lingered on her hip up to cup her breast through the fur robe, pinching her hardening nipple. The fur lining that had been so plush a moment ago became torturously stimulating. "This is my mouth on you, warm and soft, then my teeth, nipping so you squirm."

She did squirm. "Stop this. We can't."

"We can. We are." He projected an image of it, parting her robe to bare her breasts, his dark head bending over her, mouth teasing her nipples. She pressed her thighs tight together against the ache, putting her hands in his hair just as he envisioned, careful not to touch his scalp, but tugging away the leather tie he favored—the one he'd once left behind in Bára and she'd kept for him—so his curls flowed free in her grasp.

"You're avoiding the conversation about the duel," she managed as he used his grip on her hair to tug her head back, exposing her throat along with the breast he wasn't tormenting.

"Please, Arill, yes," he answered. "Spread your pretty

thighs for me, love."

"We shouldn't."

"Why not?"

She couldn't remember.

Then the door opened in the outer chamber. "Your Highness?" A voice she didn't know called out.

~ 3 ~

WITH ANOTHER GASP—NOT of the lovely sensual variety, either—Oria jumped up and drew her robe back together, retying the heavy sash. "That's why," she hissed.

Lonen's grey eyes glittered, silvery with arousal and amusement. "I *am* the king. All we have to do is tell her to go away."

"You can tell me to go, Your Highness," a woman said from the bedchamber doorway, her expression neutral, but lively curiosity in her eyes as she surveyed Oria, "but if I don't report back that you let me treat you, Prince Nolan will have Head Healer Talya in here. I understand you don't want that. Otherwise I wouldn't have interrupted."

"You're not interrupting," Oria replied, hoping her face didn't look as hot as it felt. Imagine if she'd capitulated and let Lonen continue. Worse if he'd taken it in his head to tie her to prevent accidental skin-to-skin contact—and for their mutual pleasure, as he'd discovered how well that worked for her, with those long-held and ill-advised fantasies of capture by her barbarian warrior. Yes, her face was likely bright red. She turned her back on the healer to hold her hands out to the fire, discovering Chuffta had slipped out at some point.

I'm nearby, but if you're not going to play with your mate, I'll come back. Your fire is the nicest.

Because Lonen had Alby bringing wood by the armful and the servants keeping it extra hot, for her and her Familiar both. Chuffta had wanted to mind the fire himself, but Lonen ruled that out as unwise—given the derkesthai's tendency to become obsessed with bigger and brighter—and also technically difficult, as the heavy metal screen that kept sparks from leaping out was beyond Chuffta's power to move. The possibility that the screen could be left ajar gave all the Destrye horrors. Indeed, the stone that lined the fireplaces was the only she'd seen in the otherwise wood-built palace. Lonen compensated by tasking the servants to keep the blaze burning hot at all times. A thoughtful and considerate man.

"I'm closeted with my wife," that considerate man was grumping at the healer. "There's no pressing reason to treat me right at this moment."

"On the contrary, there is concern that being upright and attending the dinner took a toll on you, Your Highness," the healer returned, calm and remorseless. "I'm tasked to give you a full examination or treatment, and that's going to happen now. Concern for the king's health trumps his commands. It's me or Talya—take your pick."

"Yes, come back," she told Chuffta, to help things along. Lonen would not stomach Talya being around either of them, not after the way the head healer had treated Oria. He might have many sterling qualities, but Lonen also held certain … 'grudges' wasn't exactly the right word. Convictions, perhaps. Okay, he was the most obstinate man she'd ever met.

"I'm upright now," Lonen pointed out, digging in, so Oria turned back. The healer met her gaze with some exasperation. She wore a lighter green veil than Talya had, and her dark hair spilled out in curls that tumbled down her back and escaped around her face in a way that reminded Oria poignantly of Juli, her waiting woman back in Bára. Though Juli's curls were red-gold, and the Destrye woman's strong frame and capable, square hands were nothing like the Báran priestess's. Her dark eyes held determination, and a clear call for action from Oria.

"Lonen," she said, moving to him and laying a hand on his shoulder so he'd look up at her. "Part of being king is making sure your people are confident and unworried. You know this. Let the healer do her job. She can only help you heal faster and grow stronger. And it will reassure your concerned brothers," she added, her tone more wry than she'd intended.

"I'm glad to hear of your confidence," he replied. "Then you'll be happy to have her do the same for the Destrye queen, too."

She opened her mouth to protest, but he'd neatly trapped her with that one.

"*I keep warning you that he's a clever man,*" Chuffta said, dropping from some vent he'd discovered and landing on her shoulder. Lonen had had the robe reinforced with padding for just that purpose, so the derkesthai's formidable talons wouldn't pierce through to her skin. Chuffta wound his long tail around her arm in affection, the iridescent white scales gleaming against the mahogany and chestnut shades of the fur. "*Probably cleverer than you are, so keep that in mind.*"

"*I shall, along with your questionable loyalty to me.*"

"*I love you best, of course,*" her Familiar replied with equanimity, "*but it's my job to avail you of my considerable wisdom.*"

She snorted with laughter and had to cover it with a cough. Though it was unlikely that the Destrye healer could do anything for her peculiar condition, this young woman possessed a compassion that Talya lacked. Maybe she'd abide by the strictures not to touch Oria, anyway. At the moment, the healer studied Chuffta, rapt with fascination. "The healer might not agree," she cautioned, speaking to the woman. "She's here for you."

The healer's dark gaze shifted to hers. "I'm willing. Please call me Baeltya."

"Agreed then. You'll treat the king first, of course."

Lonen gave her a narrow look of disbelief and she smiled back in all innocence. She'd outmaneuvered him for once.

"If you'll undress, Your Highness?" Baeltya suggested, not delaying in seizing the opportunity. She reached to help him, acting like a humble servant to the king, then narrowing her eyes, sharply noting the pained look on Lonen's face as he shrugged out of the furred vest, then lifted his arms to pull the shirt over his head. Bracing himself on the arms of the chair, he levered up, strode to the bed with a vigor made almost entirely of bravado, shucked his boots and leather pants, and stretched out naked.

Baeltya covered Lonen's groin with a towel, probably more for Oria's sake than Lonen's. Bárans weren't exactly prudes—they used communal baths, after all—but neither were they as casual of nudity as the Destrye. Or, more precisely, as Lonen was. Like all Destrye, he lived in a natural harmony with his body, and his natural confidence, an outgrowth of his exuberant presence, made him completely unselfconscious.

Oria drew up behind Baeltya in order to see better, but keeping a careful distance back. The healer kept her thoughts and emotions quite self-contained. Her native calm and reticence made her unusually restful for Oria to be around. Still, long habit and prudence had her observing a more formal space than others might. Chuffta snaked his long neck to peer at Lonen, too.

At least he'd gained back some of the weight that he'd lost

during their harrowing journey. Lonen had complained that he grew soft and fat, lolling about and not yet able to resume the strengthening exercises she'd spied upon in Bára, but there was nothing flabby about him. His chest, arm, and shoulder muscles shone with clear definition in the warm light, the sprinkling of dark hair that covered him not disguising the hardened ridges. He was every inch the massively muscled warrior she'd first encountered storming the gates of Bára.

Except for the one side of his abdomen, where the golem bite had festered. There the skin collapsed over the missing parts of him like wet silk, wrinkled and folded. If only she'd done a better job of cleaning the wound initially, when she'd had all of those fallen golems with their packets of sgath to draw from. Or if only she'd realized he hid the infection from her and acted before the corruption destroyed so much of his flesh.

She tore her eyes away from the evidence of her failure to protect the man she loved, to find his gaze waiting—granite gray and flinty with it. He watched her with steady attention and she very nearly opened her portals just a sliver to read the thoughts and feelings behind his opaque expression.

With her eyes closed, Baeltya ran her hands over Lonen's body, probing the bad side, but also pausing over his lungs and heart. Oria couldn't sense what magic—if it was magic—she used on him. Mostly it annoyed her to be both superfluous and unable to touch her husband as the healer did so casually.

As Baeltya worked, Lonen's gaze softened, going from granite to fog, the lush black lashes lowering until they draped over his broad cheekbones. His breathing deepened and mouth slackened into sleep. A soft snore dragged out of him and Baeltya stood, turning with a smile.

"There. That will help," she said.

"How is he?"

Baeltya stretched her back. "His Highness is healing, albeit slowly. Rebuilding the organs and muscle he lost to the infection simply takes time. I'll return in the morning to give him another treatment. But he needs to be resting, not meeting with his brothers, or he'll begin to backslide despite my best efforts. I'll tell Prince Nolan as much."

"No—don't," Oria said before she thought better. Nolan might push things that direction, to better his chances of winning this duel he considered.

"Or he might treat the news that Lonen is improving as a reason not to try to depose him."

"I think either way it's better for Nolan to hear Lonen is healthier than he thinks."

"And that he's not ensorcelled by you."

"Can anyone even do that?" she snapped back mentally. If so, it would be handy to ensorcell Lonen's brothers out of their doubts.

"Once you have your magic back, perhaps you can try." Chuffta's mind-voice was dry.

Baeltya had her brows raised, both for Oria's preemptory command and the silence after. Her canny dark eyes flicked to Oria's Familiar and back to her face. "I must report back my observations. That was one of my three directives."

Three? "What were the others?"

The healer gestured to Lonen. "To assess the king's health and give him a healing treatment."

"What exactly did you do?"

Baeltya spread her hands. "I am pledged to Arill, the goddess of the earth and all growing things, so I channel Her nurturing power into the patient so they can heal."

Hmm. It sounded like nonsense to Oria. If a goddess truly

existed, why would such a being care to give her power away? But if that was the Destrye analogy for magic, why hadn't she felt it?

"I didn't feel anything, either, but Lonen looks better."

Indeed, his color had returned, a healthier glow replacing the pastiness of exhaustion. He slept deeply, his body relaxed, not twitching with pain or nightmares.

"And the third part of your instructions?" Oria asked, though she suspected she knew.

Baeltya's wide mouth twitched, not quite smiling. "To assess the Báran sorceress, look for signs of enchantment, and ascertain her hold on our king."

Oria sighed mentally. Being right should be more fun. "And?"

"I haven't decided." The healer studied her. "I'll know more after I examine and treat you."

"I'm fine."

"Don't stiffen up. Part of my vows are to do no harm. Besides, you promised His Highness."

She had. Lonen must trust this woman. He'd likely thought he'd be awake for this, however. She could lie to Lonen and claim she had accepted a treatment.

Baeltya watched her, amusement sharpening her gaze. "I'll tell," she warned.

"So will I."

"You can't talk mind-to-mind with Lonen outside of the oasis.

"I have my ways."

"Traitor."

"I love you, too."

"All right then." Oria moved to the bed and drew up the fur blankets, covering Lonen to the chest, but leaving his arms outside it, as he preferred. She smoothed them over him, touching him the only way she could. Well, not quite the only. She brushed back a few of the curls rioting around his face, since she'd freed them of his hair tie. He looked so much younger in sleep, with none of the anger or bitterness war had carved into his face.

"You love him," Baeltya said, some surprise in her voice, and Oria whirled, tucking her hands behind her back as if caught by a senior priestess while looking at some illicit illustrations in the temple archives at Bára. She wasn't sure what to say—or if the healer saw something more than her gestures. Did she have something like a goddess-given version of sgath sight?

"Let's go into the other room, so we won't disturb His Highness," Oria suggested. Baeltya studied her with that discerning gaze, then nodded.

"Will you stay here with Lonen?" she asked Chuffta. *"Let me know if he stirs or needs anything."*

"Of course. I'll be right here if you need me."

The derkesthai uncoiled his tail and half-flew, half-hopped to the bed, snuggling into the furs and curling carefully against Lonen's side. Baeltya watched that, too, with the same bright interest, then led the way into the outer chamber when Oria gestured for her to. Oria pulled the door tightly closed. If Baeltya planned to make things difficult, Oria didn't want Lonen to overhear and be concerned.

"The dragonlet," Baeltya said, "he's quite intelligent."

Mentally, Oria rolled her eyes. Not as intelligent as Chuffta liked to think himself, she wanted to say.

"I heard that."

"Mind your own thoughts. And Lonen."

"I can do both of those things and mind your thoughts, as I'm so intelligent."

She contained the laugh. "He's a good companion," she temporized.

"You communicate with him somehow, don't you?" Baeltya said. "Sit here, please."

Oria sat in a chair before the smaller fire in the sitting area, keeping her expression remote. She might never have achieved true *hwil*, the perfect state of emotionlessness the priests and priestesses of Bára claimed to attain, but she had faked it well enough to fool all of them. She could easily hide her surprise—and an uneasy sense of exposure—from the Destrye healer. "Naturally. It would hardly be appropriate to keep an animal indoors if it could not follow simple rules and instructions."

Baeltya smiled, closed mouthed. "I suspect he's more of a companion to you than that."

"Is this part of your interrogation?"

The healer put her hands on her hips and sighed. "That was curiosity, and an attempt at friendly bedside manner so you'll relax. I've never met a Báran sorceress before, nor have I seen a winged lizard that seems as intelligent as our hunting hounds. Or more so. Believe it or not, my purpose—and calling—is to help."

"And to ascertain the magical hold I may or may not have on your king."

"I thought it would be better to be honest about that. Frankly I don't know how to assess such a thing if you have an agenda beyond your obvious love for him, and that he's never behaved with any woman that I know of as he does with you."

"Have you known Lon—His Highness for a long time?" She'd seen so little of this place and its people. Difficult to imagine what it had been like for Lonen, growing up here.

Baeltya smiled with some nostalgia. "We're of an age, so I first met him when I was a young apprentice and he had to be treated for a broken arm because he fell out of a tree. His sword arm, too, so his father, King Archimago, stood over him, berating him throughout the healing treatment."

"And you mended the bone?" How extraordinary.

"Not me and not entirely, but the head healer then was able to knit the bone within a week, with repeated treatments." She gave Oria an expectant look.

Fine then. "All right. Point made. What is your plan?"

"What I promised His Highness I'd do—evaluate and treat whatever problems I find as I did him." She moved toward Oria, who held up her hands to fend off the healer.

"You have to do it without touching me."

Baeltya stopped, studying her. "My art works through physical contact. I can't help you without touching you, and now the king has given me the go ahead. You don't command me. He does."

"He's asleep," Oria returned. "Or he'd back me on this. He understands."

"Understands what?"

"That you can't touch me," she said, with what she hoped sounded like patience.

"Is this some kind of Báran custom? I understand your nobility keeps far more formal practices and manners than we do." Though her voice remained neutral, Baeltya clearly found the idea off-putting. She wasn't incorrect, though those manners were driven by practical reality, not snobbery.

"It is customary—and absolute. You can't touch me."

Baeltya frowned. "I can promise that I'm objective. I don't derive sexual pleasure from it or anything like that."

The throbbing spot between her eyebrows begged to be rubbed, but Oria sat straighter to resist showing any weakness. "It's not that. There are real impacts."

"Explain this to me." The healer was as relentless as Lonen with her questions. Perhaps it was a Destrye trait.

"You wouldn't be able to understand." Oria sounded stiff and imperious to herself. Better than desperately cornered however.

"Do you need me?"

"No, I just need to find a way to make this healer go away."

"I can burn her. That always scares them."

She suppressed the smile. *"Not this time, but thank you."*

"I'm a smart woman," Baeltya was saying, her eyes snapping with offense. "I assure you I can understand a great many things, if you'll deign to explain them to this uneducated Destrye healer."

Giving in, Oria pressed her middle finger between her brows, discovering she'd broken into a fine sweat. So much for faking *hwil*. Any priestess of Bára would have spotted the cracks already. "I apologize if I gave offense." Apologizing to someone else shouldn't break Lonen's rule of one per day for each of them. And he wasn't awake to hear anyway.

Baeltya knelt beside Oria's chair, her dark eyes softer, full of sympathy. "Look. Oria. Am I saying it correctly?"

"Because you won't call me 'Your Highness'?"

The healer closed her mouth on something. "I can't. Not yet. Not without an oath of fealty. Work with me here."

"With a long 'i,'" Oria said, relenting. Talya had been vicious, but Baeltya seemed reasonably sincere. She couldn't treat them all like her enemies, not and live among them, be their queen, even, as Lonen so optimistically believed would happen. "Ohrr-eye-ahh."

"Oria," Baeltya repeated, mimicking the non-Destrye vowel twist perfectly. "I want to help you."

"You can't help me," Oria said as gently as she could. "I

simply need to eat more and regain my strength from the journey, and from being unconscious for so long."

"You've been eating, so the servants report, since you awoke and His Highness brought you from the ward for Arill's Blessings. I don't know the norm for your people, but your weight appears to be quite low, you seem to be chilled, and your skin and eyes lack luster."

"Gee, thanks," Oria bit out. "This is a cold place. And I'm sweating now."

Baeltya surveyed her. "Nerves. And something more. That's a greasy sweat from imbalance. Your system is off; I can see that much without knowing you. Why not explain to me about Bárans and touch, and see if I can do something to put you on a path toward healing?"

Her perception surprised Oria. Perhaps there was something more to her goddess-given practice than superstition.

"If I explain, will you promise not to reveal my secrets to anyone?" Oria asked.

Baeltya nodded somberly. "You didn't need to ask. My vows to Arill and my calling prevent me from revealing anyone's medical condition."

Oria raised dubious brows. "Other than your report to Prince Nolan."

"I know how to give superficial information while redacting the personal," the healer replied easily. "Now, have I passed *your* test?"

It had been one, Oria realized, and she smiled ruefully. "I apologize again. I feel…somewhat embattled here."

Baeltya smiled, full of charm. "I can only imagine. It can't be easy to have come among us under any circumstances, let alone as one of the hated enemy, near death and suspected of seducing and ensorcelling our king. Some say that you're a shapeshifter who can become one of the Trom and your pet can grow to a full-sized dragon."

Oria blinked, assimilating that. "That's quite the story."

"Oh, there's lots more rumors than that," Baeltya replied cheerfully. "How about you let me in on some of the truth?"

How to begin on such an enormous topic? "Being a sorceress means I absorb magic from the world."

Baeltya nodded encouragingly, so she continued.

"If someone touches me, it creates a kind of conduit, their skin conducts to mine and all sorts of stuff comes in. Thoughts, emotions, without filter. Depending on the sort of person they are, it can overwhelm me."

"Hmm." Baeltya looked thoughtful. "Are all Bárans like you?"

"Only the magically inclined. And I'm unusually sensitive."

"So the magically inclined don't have children—because you can't touch anyone," she reasoned.

The healer did possess a quick mind. "Your logic is sound, but there are exceptions. Some people are … better suited. Our mothers and fathers don't impact us. They're more in harmony, in a way."

"I see. So, despite the differences between our peoples, you found this harmony with His Highness and so are able to be his lover."

Oria didn't bother to correct the healer on that. If Lonen's brothers suspected the truth, that she could never fully be Lonen's lover and bear him heirs, they'd take it as one more reason to depose him. If she'd found an ideal match among her own people, she might have borne children. "There are other possibilities, too," she continued. "Some people have developed control of themselves so they don't leak nearly so much."

"Aha. Control. I'd wondered about that. Can you sense my

thoughts and emotions from there?"

"You just believe me on all of this?"

"Why would you lie?" Baeltya shrugged. "We're working on the assumption of trust here. You trust that I want to help, that I'll keep your secrets and I'll trust you in turn not to harm me and to tell me the truth."

"Harm you?"

"You're a powerful sorceress. I've heard the stories of what magics your people can wreak. I've treated many warriors returned from your walled city, wounded by forces difficult to comprehend."

It's better if they fear reprisals from you. Oria understood Lonen's reasoning there—he wanted to protect her—but she'd never wanted to be feared. "All right. At this moment, I'm not reading your thoughts and emotions. The closer you are to touching me, the more I can sense, particularly if I try."

"You can control how much you receive then?"

"Yes, to some extent." She found herself smiling. "Lonen doesn't much care for me prowling around in his head."

Baeltya grinned back. "I can just imagine. Let's try this. Over your sleeve is okay, yes?" When Oria nodded, the healer put her hand on the longer fur of the cuff of her robe, very close to the skin of her wrist. "What can you sense?"

Oria drew in a breath and allowed her senses to open ever so slightly. She wasn't as attuned to Baeltya as she was to Lonen, but the woman's presence resolved crisply and suddenly in her mind's eye. Resonant with bright green energy, her emotions shimmered like leaves in a spring storm. Sincerity, curiosity, a desire to help, a sense of urgency. Images followed: Baeltya as a girl, making her vows to the goddess, the sense of Other filling her, making her whole again. Not so alone. There she was even younger, an orphan, weeping over her parents on a farm, their bodies sliced to ribbons, livestock similarly dead and bleeding everywhere. Old, deep grief.

Oria yanked herself back, meeting the healer's calm gaze. "You were so young," she said. "The golems. Our golems—they did that, killed your family, destroyed your farm?"

Baeltya yanked her hand back as if burned. "You saw all of that?"

"I'm sorry. When I said I can control it, that's an exaggeration. Sometimes I see more than I mean to. I didn't intend to invade your privacy."

"No, it's all right." Baeltya rubbed her fingertips together. "I wanted to show you what the goddess-sent healing feels like. The rest must be attached to that."

"Strong emotions can be that way," Oria agreed. "Tied to old memories. We can stop there."

"No, no—that was a first step. To find the baseline, if you will. Now I want to try something else." Baeltya closed her eyes as she had with Lonen, stilling herself. Her presence drew back palpably. Much like a Báran meditating to nourish a state of *hwil*, Oria realized with a sense of dislocation. The Destrye knew of such practices? But how, and why did the temple—

"All right," Baeltya broke into her whirling thoughts, her voice even, slightly remote, "I'll touch your sleeve again."

She did. Oria waited for the return of the Destrye woman's presence and memories.

"Anything?"

"No." How curious. Not even a breath of that green vibrant energy.

"I'm going to touch your skin. Tell me if it pains you."

"Believe me," Oria replied, bracing herself for the agonizing onslaught, "you'll know."

Baeltya smiled slightly, then slowly moved her hand onto

Oria's. Anticipating the jolt of searing invasion she'd experienced before, Oria jumped a little at the shock of contact. The healer opened her eyes in concern, but didn't move. "Yes? No?"

To her astonishment, Oria felt nothing from the woman. Just a warm hand on her skin and a hint of something, like the faint scent of the inside of a leaf. "That's amazing. I'm fine. How did you do that?"

"I kind of reversed what I normally do, so I wouldn't flow into you. Now I'm going to see if I can do an assessment without changing that flow. Is that all right?"

Oria relaxed back, stunned to feel so reassured by the soothing contact. "Yes. Go ahead."

The healer's energy flowed through her, but without invasion. Like a soft evening breeze that sifted over her skin, but never stirred her hair. In its wake, warmth lingered behind, a hint of the desert sun Oria missed in her very bones, along with a kind of well-being she hadn't felt since her father died and her mother collapsed. She nearly melted into the chair with the sweet surcease of it.

"You're starving."

At Baeltya's words, Oria forced open her heavy eyelids to find the Destrye healer standing before her, rubbing her hands together in a way Oria recognized—a method for shedding accumulated magic.

"Why are you starving?" the healer mused, almost to herself. "I've done what I can for you, and you napped for a bit which did you good, but you're going to have to help me here. We don't have much food, what with the rationing, but you clearly need more than you're getting. Or do you need a different kind of food?"

"I don't think any kind of food will help," Oria told her. At least whatever the healer had done for her helped fend off the specter of despair.

"Oria—I'm not sure you understand. I've seen people who've starved to death who weren't as far gone as you are. We need to take action or you won't last much longer."

"How much longer?" Lonen asked from the doorway, startling Oria. She hadn't heard him open the door. Nor had Chuffta warned her.

"You were sleeping. It was good for you."

Lonen strode in, barefooted, wearing only his leather pants, his hair hanging down his back, and took Baeltya by the shoulders. "Tell me straight. How much longer?"

<h1 style="text-align:center">~ 4 ~</h1>

HE MISSED ORIA immediately when he awoke, knowing with some deep sense he'd acquired that she wasn't in the room. The warm weight nestled against his side stirred, and Chuffta lifted his head, emerald green eyes shining like jewels in his narrow, triangular face. He'd liked being able to hear the derkesthai's thoughts—snotty as they'd been at the time—because reading the expression in that reptilian gaze wasn't easy. As if understanding, which he might, Chuffta cocked his head and lifted his wings in a very human-seeming shrug.

Lonen chuckled and lifted a tentative hand to scratch the spot between the golden horns that curved out of Chuffta's head and rub the surprisingly soft white ears that flanked them. The derkesthai leaned into his hand, making a rumbling sound of pleasure that sounded much like a cat's purr. Not an easy spot for Chuffta to reach, that little valley, Oria had explained, and Lonen could see why. After a moment, though, Chuffta pulled away and looked at the door. A murmur of feminine voices where there had been silence.

"Best see what's up, eh, Chuffta buddy?" He levered himself up, feeling considerably less winded, his side moving more easily as he pulled on his pants. He could be the better man and admit they'd been right about treating him. That would be the answer to ending this enforced inaction. He needed to get into top form—okay, at least working condition—to find Oria a sustaining source of magic.

The rest could wait, Arill take them.

Opening the door, he heard the tail end of the conversation, words that chilled his blood. *...or you won't last much longer.*

"How much longer?" he demanded. Oria whirled in the big chair that dwarfed her slight frame, her mass of hair crackling, strands rising with static like the flames leaping behind her, copper eyes enormous in her white face. So much thinner. He'd noticed it before, but her unusual appearance always struck him as exotically beautiful. Now he could see how her high cheekbones stood out like knife blades, her skin seeming nearly transparent enough for them to cut through. Seeing her clearly, without the fog of love and relief at having her alive and with him, filled him with rage that he'd been allowing himself to live in a fantasy the last few days.

Does nothing dim your optimism?

Apparently, a dose of reality from a healer did. Baeltya's eyes widened, though not in alarm—concern?—as he took hold of her and asked how much longer.

"I can't answer that," she said.

He resisted the urge to shake the truth out of the woman. Baeltya had the sheen of Arill about her, as all the best healers did. She knew more than she let on.

"Can't or won't?" he snarled.

"Lonen." Oria was beside him, hand hovering next to his arm, where normally she'd touch him if he'd remembered to put on a shirt. "Baeltya helped me. She can touch me without harm. Don't break her." A smile ghosted around her lips.

He let go of the healer. "I didn't hurt her," he grumbled.

"Wait—she could touch you?"

"Yes." Oria nodded with a broad smile. "Something to do with her healer's control, like our *hwil*."

"Is this something I can learn?" he demanded of Baeltya. The possibilities whirled in his mind, while the healer gaped, clearly thrashing for an answer to the odd question from her king.

"It would involve meditating, no doubt," Oria teased him. At least some of her mischievous spirit had returned.

"To lie with you, I'd learn even that," he told her with fervor, and she shifted, flicking a cautious glance at Baeltya. "Fine. We'll pursue that later. I want my straight answer."

Baeltya held up her palms, unruffled. "I can't answer, not won't. Oria isn't just foreign, she's different from the Destrye in many ways. Her physiology and energy feel unlike anything I've encountered before. I'd hesitate to predict anything with her."

"But you said you could compare her to other patients, who you knew to be starving."

Baeltya frowned in thought. "Yes, I can discern that much, though even that is odd. She 'feels' malnourished to me on both those physiological and energetic levels. I don't understand it."

"Then you should have a sense of how long she has."

"I don't. I have some ideas that might—"

"Stop hedging, healer. How long?"

"She should be dead already!" Baeltya snapped. "If she were Destrye, she would be."

It took a moment for his stricken heart, to catch up to a regular beat. "You have to help her."

"I am working on it, Your Highness."

"Enough of this," Oria put in with some asperity, her voice

cutting. "I do happen to be standing right here. I'm not one of your horses that you can be debating whether it's too ill to be put down."

"Of course not, love," he said, with some chagrin. Baeltya noticed the endearment, drawing in a breath, and looking between them. Better to make that clear, too. He'd kept them closeted too long. His people—and his family—would soon learn that he would not budge on his feelings, or on Oria's place in his life. He'd abdicate first, if they forced him into it. "I apologize."

Oria smiled at him, copper eyes soft with an affectionate glow she reserved only for him and Chuffta. "There's *your* one for the day. Baeltya, you said you have ideas? I feel much better for your treatment, so I'd like to hear them."

"Well, let's start with the prosaic. Do you normally eat anything that you're not eating now?"

Oria's smile quirked a bit to the side. "That's an easy yes. Almost nothing here is what I ate before."

"Like what?"

"I never ate meat before this. Bárans eat lots of fruits, leafy greens, vegetables, grains. We do eat bread, like you do."

Baeltya cast him a look, making him feel abruptly like a careless boy again rather than King of the Destrye. "Why haven't you ordered these foods brought to her?"

"Meat is good for her," he grumbled. Arill knew he'd gone to enough trouble to force it down her stubborn throat. Now that he had her compliant on the matter, he'd kept up with it. Meat built muscle and bone, didn't it?

Baeltya sighed heavily for his idiocy, putting her hands on hips and shaking her head. "Your Highness," she began, as if using his title again would mitigate the scolding to come, "a person who's spent her entire life, whose physiology for generations—" she cast a glance at Oria for confirmation.

"At least," Oria replied.

"Whose physiology for many generations is acclimatized or even adapted to extracting nourishment from non-meat sources, cannot simply go to an all-meat diet and thrive on it. Her body isn't set up to process it effectively."

"It hasn't been all meat," he said in his defense, though really there wasn't any. "There's been bread, too."

Oria laced her fingers together. "I mainly eat the bread," she confided, and Baeltya threw up her hands.

"What?" Lonen stared at her. "What about all the meat I give you?"

She lifted her chin in defiance. "I can't eat all that. It makes my stomach hurt, so I slip it onto your plate when you're not looking. You need it, too."

He processed that, stunned. "Oria, if you think—"

"Arill save us," Baeltya interrupted. "All right, at least this I can do. It's the wrong season for leafy greens, but we do have stores of various grains, root vegetables, and dried fruits. What about fruit juices?"

"I would kill for some fruit juice," Oria replied with fervor.

Lonen absorbed her bright-eyed enthusiasm with a growing sense of betrayed injury. "Why didn't you tell me? You know I'd give you anything you asked for."

Baeltya cleared her throat. "I'm going to step out for a moment and get a nourishing meal on its way while you two sort this out."

Oria thanked her and waited for the outer door to close, returning her somber gaze to his. "Let's sit." She went back into the bedchamber and took her accustomed place by the bigger fire, curling her bare feet up under her, tucking them beneath the hem of the furry robe. Chuffta had also returned to his nest before the fire, the fine tip of his tail tapping in welcome, though he otherwise didn't move. The both of them, still adjusting to the cold. And it wasn't even deep winter yet. For himself, he left his shirt off as he sat, the fire almost too hot for him. A small sacrifice to make.

"Lonen," she began, twisting her fingers together, "this is a strange place for me to be."

"I know Dru is different, but you'll get used to it. You've barely seen this land. Wait until I show it to you."

"It's not that." She shook her head slightly, then tucked a heavy lock of her shining copper hair behind one ear. "I mean, I look forward to seeing Dru. From the few leaves I've seen, the trees must be enormous. And lakes! I want to see those, too. No, I mean, it's strange for me to be in this position where absolutely everything I need comes through you. Food, clothing, this fire, healing. My very life depends on you and I don't … like asking for more."

"You don't like it," he echoed, feeling a dangerous edge, though he tried to contain it.

She eyed him warily, far too sensitive to his moods. "Don't get angry."

"I'm not." Though he was and they both knew it. "Let me ask you this—how can I know what you need if you don't *like* asking for it?"

Her eyes flashed hot copper. "Don't pull attitude with me, Lonen. I'm trying to be honest here."

He flung himself out of the chair, pacing off the surge of … okay, anger. First his cursed brothers, now this. "Since you're being so honest, how about telling me why in Arill you still don't trust me? I thought we were past this. You're my *wife*, Arill take you. You know I love you; you say you love me. We're in this together. You're not dependent on me. Everything I have is already yours. Why can't you understand that?"

She had her face averted, and Chuffta raised his head, looking to her. She gazed back at her Familiar as they clearly exchanged some confidences, ones that left him out. "What does Chuffta say?" he demanded.

Oria transferred her gaze to him, her eyes pooled with unshed tears. "That you're a boor and a brute of a barbarian Destyre warrior and I'm better off without you!"

Lonen clenched his fists and growled. "He said no such thing."

"Then why did you bother to ask?" she snapped at him, tucking herself deeper into the chair and hugging herself.

"Oria." The anger drained out of him, like water lost from a broken vessel. He dropped to the rug at her feet and laid his head on her fur-covered knees, wrapping his arms behind her slim hips. "I am a boor and a brute. I'm sorry."

Her fingers drifted through his hair, soothing with the relief the caress brought him. "You're not. I shouldn't have said so. I'm sorry, too. There—we're even with each of us over by one for the day."

"Then we'll have to be sure to do nothing to apologize for tomorrow."

"That would be good," she said softly.

"I thought everything would be okay," he said, rubbing his cheek against the fur, "if we could just get to Dru. Back in the desert, even the oasis, I just felt so certain that, once here, we'd be all right, that everything would fall into place."

"There's your rosy optimism coming into play," she replied, though she didn't sound scornful with it. "I love that about you, Lonen, I really do. But things don't end as in the tales. There's no happy ever after in real life. There's just the ending of that time of trial, and then the people go on to face new trials. We maybe don't usually hear that part of the story, so we forget it."

He lifted his head, resting his chin on her knees, looking up at her. "We can go back to the oasis. You at least weren't starving for magic there."

"You said it wasn't sustainable—no game coming in, no fruits on the trees, or other food to gather."

"We'll take food with us. Chuffta and I can go hunt in the desert."

"And we'll do what? Just hang out and do nothing all day?"

"And have sex. Lots and lots of sex," he reminded her, massaging her back through the robes. "We can touch there."

A light, pretty flush graced her cheekbones. "Besides that. We married for duty, to serve our peoples, not to run off and indulge ourselves in sex."

"The latter is sounding better to me all the time."

"Be serious, Lonen—we have responsibilities. You said it yourself."

He regretted that, too. It had seemed so urgent to get them back to Dru, to save the Destrye. "That was before I knew Nolan had survived. He can be king instead. I never wanted it. He does."

"Nolan can't fight Yar or the Trom," Oria said gently, her expression oddly compassionate as she brushed a curl back from his forehead. His hair tie was around there somewhere. "You know that as well as I do. No matter what your brothers think, we both know this war isn't over."

"I can't fight them without you." The ache grabbed his throat. "Without you I won't even want to."

"Don't say that," she whispered. "You're not a man who stops fighting, not for any reason. Look how far we've made it. That's all because of you and your determination to get us here to Dru."

True. And part of that had determination had also been to save Oria. Maybe that had been rosy optimism, but he'd believed Arill's healers could help her, that she could find magic here. That they'd triumph. Somewhere, deep in his heart, he still believed that.

"You're going to get better," he told her.

She looked amused. "Is that an order, Your Highness?"

"It is, Your Highness."

"I take it you two have made up?" Baeltya said from the doorway. She had the grace to look slightly abashed at Lonen's glare. Healers claimed a certain autonomy that let them skirt even the more relaxed protocols of the Destrye nobility, but cheekiness went a bit far. "That is, the food is on its way, Your Highness, Oria."

"Your Highnesses," Lonen corrected.

Baeltya edged into the room. "Not under Destrye law, King Lonen."

"A formality only."

"A critical one," Baeltya pointed out. "And not my purview. Oria's health is, so let's discuss the energetic aspect of her condition."

He deferred to Oria on that one, who was naturally discussing it with her Familiar. She got a certain look in her eye when she did, an unfocused distraction that gave her away. Not that he'd reveal how he could tell, as it gave him a rare window into the thoughts of his sorceress wife.

Her focus returned to him. "Baeltya says I can trust her with my secrets."

It was a question for him. He stood, pulling on his shirt while he thought. Arill's healers did take a vow of confidentiality, but there were also plenty of stories throughout history of healers helping various political factions with the potent information they extracted. Without studying Baeltya outright, he considered her and checked his gut feeling about the junior healer. He'd picked her to attend him because she wasn't Talya—not necessarily a strong recommendation—and because her calm and steady reserve reminded him of Juli, who'd been good for Oria—which might be as good a recommendation as any.

"Oria has explained her skin sensitivity to me, and that it's part of her absorbing magic from the world," Baeltya said evenly, catching his eye. "I can guess that if she is starving energetically, that's because she's not able to absorb what she needs here in Dru, because we have no magic here."

"That's true," Oria said, not flinching when he narrowed his eyes at her in warning. "If it's a choice between trusting her and maybe living or not trusting anyone and dying, I'm going to take the risk." Her eyes held the knowledge of the same feelings he'd confessed to her. She wouldn't necessarily act to save herself, but she'd gallop headlong into every battle in order to save him.

He folded his arms and leaned against the mantel. "Go on, then. It's up to you to decide what to tell."

She nodded at him, her expression soft as a kiss, then spoke to Baeltya. "You do have magic here. It's everywhere, arising from all living things, pushed and pulled by the moons as they wax and wane. But here it's what we call wild magic. It's... chaotic. Very strong but also in a form I can't digest, to compare it to food."

"Like deer can eat bark but we can't, because our guts aren't set up for it," Baeltya supplied, thoroughly intrigued, judging by the light in her dark eyes.

"That makes sense. Only imagine the tree falling on you

because you can't eat it. In Bára, we had a source of purified magic, called sgath, that we could all draw on."

"How did it get purified?"

Oria glanced at Chuffta, silent a moment. Then shook her head slightly "We don't know."

"We?" Baeltya pounced on that. "You *can* communicate with it."

"You Destrye and your 'its,'" Oria laughed, holding out an arm to her Familiar. He hopped up, craning his neck with interest at the healer. "His name is Chuffta. He's a derkesthai and, yes, I can talk to him mind-to-mind. He's slightly smarter than your hunting hounds. Ow!" She pulled her hair from Chuffta's mouth where he yanked on it. "Okay, much smarter. You can touch him, if you like."

Baeltya's face went reverent as she ran a finger down Chuffa's arched neck, and Lonen remembered that feeling well. He'd expected the scales to be hard and slick, not soft as talc. "As smart as we are?" she asked.

"Different," Oria hedged. "Don't you bite me. You know it's true. He is similarly intelligent, though he sees the world differently. His kind tell stories to transmit history, rather than recording them in books."

"Oral histories." Baeltya's shrewd gaze flicked to Lonen. "Once the Destrye were the same. Barbarians telling tales around the campfires."

"We've progressed in any number of ways since then," Lonen pointed out.

"And not in others," Baeltya retorted.

"A work in progress," he agreed without rancor. Oria looked back and forth between them, filing the information away in her own keen memory.

"So," Baeltya returned to business, still stroking Chuffta,

who tipped back his chin for a scratching there from the healer's adept fingers. "You said, 'we don't know,' meaning you and Chuffta. He advises you?"

"Yes, he's my Familiar. He helps me manage chaotic magical input, gives me advice, and is my oldest friend. Neither of us knows how the sgath came to be below Bára, except that the part of the duties of any priestess is to take sgath she absorbs and feed it into the common pool."

Baeltya frowned. "That's circular. You pull it from this source and also put it back?"

Oria looked thoughtful. "I never thought of it in those terms. Some things you just grow up thinking you know, and then when you step back and evaluate them through other eyes, they don't make sense."

"I think that's part of becoming an adult," Baeltya replied, glancing at Lonen again with wry amusement, then away, as if remembering herself.

"Maybe one day I'll find out," he commented and Oria rolled her eyes.

"So, maybe you can purify the wild magic, create your own reservoir here," Baeltya prompted. "If you knew how to input to the one in Bára, you should have the instinct and ability."

Oria blanched at the mention of accessing the wild magic, a glimmer of fear she so rarely evinced. "I think… that is not an option," she said softly.

"Maybe you can find a way to both cushion the effect on yourself and then purify and store it. It seems someone in your ancestry must have done that in the first place."

"Oh yes? You sound very confident of that. Is that how your Arill-delivered healing happened? A priestess woke up one day and said, 'hey, I think I'll meditate a whole bunch and see if Arill will give me some of her divine power!'" Oria's eyes flashed with emotion as she said it, so Lonen didn't laugh, knowing that her fear spoke.

Baeltya regarded her steadily. "Actually the legend is pretty close to that. I'll tell it to you some day."

If he'd expected her to apologize to the healer again, she didn't. Instead she firmed her chin. "I'd be interested to hear that. It would be helpful if I had a similar legend to work off of. Everything I've been told is that wild magic means death—fast or slow—but death."

"Overload on one hand, or starvation because you shut it out?"

Oria inclined her head in acknowledgment, a rueful twist to her mouth—that became a smile for her Familiar. "Chuffta says the problem with humans is that we're too black and white, that it's not always one thing or another."

"So, is there another option?"

"There's one." Oria's coppery eyes, dark now with consideration, looked to his. "Though that solution has a number of moving parts also."

"We'll discuss that," he told her, certain she contemplated some plan of enticing golems through the recently discovered tunnels so she could steal the packets of sgath they carried. Perhaps the danger of that truly would be less than her wrestling the wild magic, but he knew fighting golems from personal experience. His side throbbed with the memory and the scar over his eye twitched. He wanted Oria far from the lethal creatures. "A possible back up plan, but even you have to admit it's far from a long-term solution."

"Then it's back to you purifying wild magic into a sgath source like you had in Bára," Baeltya pointed out in all practicality.

"It is some sort of cycle," Oria mused. "We've been wondering if the source in Bára has something to do with that underground lake."

"That Prince Nolan nearly drowned in?" Baeltya raised her brows. "That would be interesting. Though we have no underground lake here that I know of."

"We have other lakes." And he would take Oria to one. He should have thought of it sooner.

"Lake Scandamalion is a day's journey from here," Baeltya pointed out. "It's the closest with any water left in it."

"And that's not the one I have in mind." No, he'd take her to Lake Chenault, his favorite. If they only had a little time left—*don't think of it*—well, he wanted her to at least see it.

"Surely you're not thinking of going to—"

"Where I go is my business, healer. I'll remind you of your vows."

"Your Highness," Baeltya gave Chuffta one last caress and held up her palms in surrender. "Is that wise?" Her question held a volume of unspoken information.

"It's not," Oria put in crisply. "You cannot leave the palace now. Not with all that's going on."

"I am king," he told his wife, ignoring the healer. "I decide what I can and cannot do."

"Don't pull out your 'hear my manly roar' bluster with me." Oria glared at him. "You might be a barbarian, but you don't frighten me."

"Maybe I haven't tried hard enough," he replied in a tone as silken as the robes she once wore.

Baeltya looked between them and, apparently deciding they were done, scrubbed her palms together. "I'm going to check on that meal. I think I heard the servants."

"Besides," Oria continued, "you have no idea if *your* plan

would work either. Neither you nor I know where to begin."

"I actually do have an idea on that." One he'd been nursing for some time. If his memory served him correctly, he might have something of a place to start. "For tonight, though, you eat the food Baeltya has arranged. We'll sleep. Tomorrow, after another round of treatments, I will introduce you to my brothers, show you to the people, and settle matters there. The day after, if the healer approves, and if we've thought of nothing else, we'll set out on our journey."

"I agree that we'll talk about possibilities more then."

"There's but one viable possibility, if you're not too stubborn to see it."

"I don't know about this, Lonen."

"Trust me." He'd meant it to be firm, but an edge of a plea filtered in.

"I do." She trailed long fingers down Chuffta's back. "I promise that I do."

As much as she trusted in anything anymore.

$$\sim 5 \sim$$

T HE FOOD DID help. The fruit juice, in particular, sank like a balm to some dried-out core of her, saturating her desiccated soul. Though the root vegetables were somewhat wizened, they still tasted nourishing, particularly with the salted cream that Lonen dolloped on the starchier ones for her. She hesitated to eat too much, thinking of how lean the Destrye stores must be, but Lonen gave her such a threatening scowl that she didn't voice it. With her belly finally full in a satisfying way instead of a gut-cramping one, she grew sleepy.

Lonen was groggy, too, from the healing nap, so they crawled under the furs together, the room lit only by the fire, and fell asleep. With Lonen's arm draped over her hips over the thick, quilted nightgown she wore, she slept deeply.

For a while.

Until the wild magic invaded her dreams, that was.

At first she thought she lived her life as she always had—which should have clued her in, because her life had become anything but normal. All of that was shattered and gone.

But the dream worked on her so she forgot all that, walking among the flowers and hanging vines of her rooftop terrace, atop her tower in Bára. The blue desert sky arced above, cloudless and hot. All around, the towers of Bára rose in fanciful spires, capped and scrolled in the colors of the sun.

Chuffta preened on the carved balustrade, a shimmering white so bright she squinted against his brilliance. He looked at her, the green of his eyes almost painful.

"Don't forget what I am, Oria. Or what you are."

She paused, trying to remember how to reply mentally, but her brain felt mute, stuffed with silk.

As she struggled to move, to think, trapped and mesmerized, the reptilian black slits of the small dragon's pupils widened, expanding so his eyes became matte pits that consumed his narrow head. His skull and body swiftly caught up. Then his eyes grew. Then the body and wings again, leapfrogging each other. He swelled until he filled the terrace, and beyond, overlapping the balustrade, squeezing her out, until she hung perilously over the precipice, pinned between the abyss of the city and his black eyes, now larger than herself.

"Don't forget," his mind-voice grated over her brain, burning into it, setting her on fire with its leaf-dry, knife-edged hiss. *"You've taken not one, but several steps farther down your path."*

"No." Her mouth muffled it, refusing to work, just like her mind. "No!" she tried again, pushing out the shout that was only a mutter.

"We come when summoned. Don't forget."

"Never!" She arched away, the dizzying drop threatening to devour her. "I won't."

"You will. Queen Ponen. Don't forget."

"Let me go!" She screamed it, wrenching away, and fell. She plummeted from the tower, stretching her arms to become wings, wild magic swirling in, exploding her body, transforming her into a dragon so black she became a hole in the sky.

She burned with the power. Arching her neck, she trumpeted it to the sky. Fire, thick and turbulent, welled up like vomit, billowing from her lips. She screamed her triumph after it, the coal of terror sending agony through her heart.

Burn!

"Oria!" A stinging slap to her cheek brought with it a searing impression of Lonen—and a font of his emotions slamming through her. Anger. Despair. Terror. Love. Desperation. The tumult shook her, but also made sense, human sense, in a way the wild magic didn't. "Arill, take you, Oria, wake up!"

"I'm awake!" she gasped. Then gasped again, dragging at the air. She couldn't breathe.

"Lonen is sitting on you." Chuffta's mind-voice—his real mind-voice—fluted through her head, real and reassuring, too.

Lonen leaned close to her face, looming over her, a shaggy, wild silhouette against the dimming fire. He had her pinned by the wrists, thighs clamped on either side of her hips, his weight crushing. "Breathe!" he demanded.

"Get. Off. Me." She managed while struggling to draw breath.

In a flash, he was off her. Off the bed. Now a standing, naked silhouette between her and the blazing torches of the Destrye guards who'd pounded down the door and poured into the bedchamber, Alby in the lead.

"Your Highness!" Alby skidded to a halt. "What—"

"Stand down," Lonen said, voice gravelly, but firm. "There is no danger. Go."

"But Your Highness—"

"Go!" he thundered. The boom of his rage echoed through his voice, making her flinch. She sat up and Alby's eyes fell on her, wide and startled. Then he and the men saluted and fled, Lonen following after, practically chasing them out.

"I would never push you off a tower." Chuffta sat on the carved wooden footboard, gripping with his talons, head

cocked in question. His mind-voice had a hesitant sound. *"Or say those things."*

"I know," she replied aloud, too frenetic and drained to try for the concentration of replying mentally. She held out a hand to him and he hopped onto the blankets, hop-flying onto her lap, coiling his tail around her wrist and helping to relieve the pressure of the magic and the aftertaste of the nightmare. "It was only a dream."

"Not only."

"Only?" Lonen echoed Chuffta unintentionally, striding back into the room, carrying a hammered metal cup that glinted in the low light. "That was the goddess of all night-mares."

"You're one to talk," she muttered.

Lonen crawled up onto the bed, steadying the cup as he did, then handed it to her, concern creasing his shadowed face. "Yes—thus I know what I'm talking about. Drink this."

The liquor, sweet and bright, burned in her throat as the fire had in her dream.

"It doesn't really burn like that, breathing fire," Chuffta noted. *"Your throat hurts because you were screaming."*

"I was screaming?"

Lonen raked a hand through his hair. "Froze the blood in my veins so the lumps nearly stopped my heart. You took years off my life, love. What in Arill brought that on?"

The wild magic. Perhaps the conversation had suggested it, or opening her portals to Baeltya had made her more vulnerable. The narrowing of her senses that had allowed her to shut out the wild magic instead of absorbing it was far from a practiced skill or a precise art. She opened her mouth to apologize for waking him, for bringing the guards running, then remembered that, even if it was after midnight, she'd already used up her apology for that day, too. Not sure what else to say, she closed her mouth again.

"Talk to me, Oria," Lonen growled. "Let's not rehash this."

"I don't always know the answers to your questions." She'd wanted to snap out that reply, but it dribbled wearily.

"But you know this one. Even I can guess. It's the wild magic, isn't it? You're vulnerable to it no matter what. It invades your sleep, when your guard is down. Just as happened on the journey here."

Oria took a long swallow of the liquor. It burned less this time. "I didn't realize you knew about that."

"I knew. I just didn't say anything." He slid his fingers through the hair that spilled over her shoulder, tugging a little when he met a tangle. She must have been thrashing in her sleep, too, as well as screaming.

"I don't know *how* you knew." She met his steady gray gaze.

"The pair of us, both restless in our dreams—one recognizes the other. I only guessed." He said so, but her jangling sensitivity to him showed it to be a lie. Not maliciously told, but the visceral truth nevertheless pulsed along the marital bond between them. He *knew*. Lonen somehow accessed some deeper knowledge about her, something she hadn't expected from their alliance. Were all temple-joined marriages like this? She didn't think so. She'd never heard any of the priests and priestesses even in ideal marriages speak of this kind of subconscious *knowing*. Of course, given how Yar had treated Gallia, who was supposed to be his ideal bride, like a trophy, it would be difficult to imagine him being sensitive to much about her at all. Also, the priests and priestesses weren't given to spilling any intimate secrets.

With a nearly physical pang, she abruptly missed her

mother with a deep and desperate longing. Rhianna would have answered her questions.

"Maybe. She didn't always. And the influence of the Trom is unprecedented, at least in recent memory. Odd how their words invaded your dream."

She really hoped Lonen hadn't witnessed any details of the dream as Chuffta had. Though normally Chuffta didn't comment on her dreaming thoughts.

"Because I don't usually hear them. When you sleep, I hear you in my mind, but without focus. As if you're very far away. This was different."

As if it hadn't really been a dream at all. Lonen still gazed at her, as if reading her thoughts in her eyes, his fingers wound in her hair, stroking one lock caught between his thumb and forefinger. "Yes, I think the wild magic gave me that … nightmare." She offered that like a confession.

He tugged her hair with affection and shrugged as if none of it mattered a great deal. "I think you have no choice," he put to her, rising and fetching another goblet.

"No choice?" About him seeing the inside of her head?

"About confronting the wild magic," he said. "Even if you went ahead with this unlikely plan to lure golems through the tunnels so you could steal their sgath, the wild magic will continue to work on you any time your defenses are down. You have no choice but to learn to manage it somehow."

"Or learn to improve my subconscious controls so they stay in place when I sleep." That seemed far more feasible.

"You have a plan for that?" He drank deeply, head thrown back to drain the liquor, the column of his throat strong beneath his neat beard.

"You know I don't."

He smiled slightly, a quirk of shadow in the flickering firelight. "We proceed with the plan then. We cannot ignore the wild magic, so we'll have to face it."

She didn't at all like the sound of that. "You mean I will."

"No, *we* will. We're in this together."

She had no immediate argument. Not a coherent one. "We already agreed that we'd talk about it more tomorrow."

Tossing aside the empty goblet and taking hers, Lonen slid under the furs again, snugging her against him. "We can talk all you like, love—within the deadline we already agreed to— but it seems there will be no escaping this truth." Despite his uncompromising words and tone, his touch soothed, his empathy for her fears shimmered in her heart, a shining and solid comfort.

"You're always so sure things will turn out well," she accused, but drowsiness—and the warmth of his nearness— softened her words.

"One day you'll accept that I'm always right." He kissed her hair.

Rather than arguing, or giving him the satisfaction of agreeing, she focused on shutting her portals tight, before let herself fall back to sleep. The morning would be soon enough to examine the walls of the trap she found herself in.

As if they'd broken a seal on the oasis of Lonen's chambers with a three-part ritual—Lonen going out to dine with his brothers, admitting Baeltya, and the inrush of guards brought by her night terrors—with the advent of daylight, the outside world began pouring in. And much like the cracks in her mental and emotional portals let in the wild magic, the Destrye brought chaos of all levels with them.

The morning began serenely enough. Lonen was already up when she awoke, doing some stretching and strengthening exercises before the fire, which she took as a good sign. Baeltya soon arrived, along with a hearty breakfast of stewed fruit and grains. More healing treatments and a nap in the chair by the fire fast gave way to a thorough invasion of her sanctuary. Women of all stations, it seemed, arrived with various supplies and implements—dresses, clothes, grooming aids, advice—all of which seemed to be more excuses to look her over with their critical dark eyes.

Lonen, the traitor, abandoned her with a kiss to the top of her head and a whisper to have courage. The way he kept his expression deliberately neutral, though his mouth crooked at the corners suspiciously, told her all she needed to know about how seriously he took the female attack. Since he went to be briefed on the situation facing Dru, she supposed her own troubles paled in comparison.

Still, it was her first real encounter with the women of the Destrye court, and she knew full well these situations were quicksand of their own variety.

Even Chuffta fled the center of the scene, taking a perch on a high beam and watching with a keen-eyed gaze, making laconic comments in her mind, which she studiously ignored. Lonen might insist that the Destrye conducted themselves far less formally than Bárans, and he'd be largely correct, but the female politics seemed uncannily akin to the undercurrents of temple jockeying for power and position, all under the serene guise of *hwil*.

These women, however, made no pretense of any sort of emotional control. At first they whispered and murmured to each other, but once they determined that Oria couldn't follow the twisty Destrye dialect, they spoke more boldly, chattering amongst themselves and occasionally erupting into passionate arguments—once over the difference between two spools of thread, to all appearances. For her part, Oria took the opportunity to observe their ways, while concentrating on sustaining her own *hwil* that also served to keep her portals tightly closed.

They were careful, at least, in not touching her. The seamstresses laid their measuring tapes over her light bed gown. Lonen, or Baeltya, had passed the word and they observed the protocol scrupulously, whatever they might believe to be the reason for it. Several maids staggered in heaped with furs, leathers, and some heavier materials that gleamed with deep color, and the seamstresses fell into animated discussion that seemed to involve how best to use the fur as lining.

Apparently Lonen intended to see her warmly clothed, a tremendous relief. The ladies had returned her fur robe to her and one indicated a metal pot of something hot warmed over a candle flame encased in a metal-screened box. Oria nodded and the girl, younger than the others, with eyes of a blue that reminded Oria of the flowers that bloomed only in the first cool of morning, poured her a mug. Oria sat by the fire, cupping it in her hands to warm them. The pot was of a hammered coppery metal that caught the light, making her blush to recall the times Lonen had brushed her hair, praising the sheen and color. The liquid seemed to be a brew of fragrant flowers and perhaps a spicy bark. It warmed her from the inside out, leaving behind a sense of bright well-being, which made her wonder if it came from Baeltya.

Like jewelbirds when a raptor flies over, the chattering women fell suddenly silent, bowing their heads as a tall woman entered the room. She wasn't particularly richly dressed, but she carried herself like a high priestess or queen. Unlike the other women, she wore her hair short against her scalp, the curls in black whorls against her lighter skin. Without the elaborate fall of coiled hair like the others, her deep blue eyes stood out large under arched dark brows. They held a solemnity echoed by her full lips, both bracketed by etched lines of grief.

She studied Oria with bold appraisal, not acknowledging the silent women around her. Oria fought the urge to rise to her feet, or even make obeisance. Lonen had been quite clear that he expected her to conduct herself as the Queen of the Destrye. The battle would not be that easy, of course, but if Oria had learned little else, she knew that faking the appearance of station took one a great deal of the way to actually having it. So she stared back at the woman, her own face a mask of perfect *hwil*, raising her brows ever so slightly in inquiry, as her mother would do. The woman seemed to wait for something more and Oria mentally cursed Lonen for insisting there were no particular protocols to learn.

Men could be so obtuse.

"Human males," Chuffta corrected with a hint of a sniff. *"I am most perceptive."*

"Can you read anything from her?"

"She is very sad. And angry. Also, surprised by you."

Oria had no opportunity to follow that up, because the woman spoke, her voice surprisingly deep. "I am Salaya," she said, in Common Tongue.

"I am Oria," she replied, using the same phrasing and intonation. Lonen likely would have wanted her to add "Queen of the Destrye," but that felt like too much of a declaration of war with this hard-eyed woman. Who was she? Salaya. She didn't recall hearing the name spoken. At least she wasn't Natly, but

Salaya's unfriendly demeanor didn't bode much better.

Salaya said nothing more, but neither did Oria offer anything further. Something else she knew—how to wait out a high priestess who hoped for the least lapse in *hwil* to pounce upon as further proof of Oria's deep unsuitability. If Salaya thought to intimidate with brooding silence then she'd be in for further surprises. Oria had withstood worse.

"You're a bit of a thing," Salaya finally said. "I imagine I could break you in two with my bare hands."

Oria smiled thinly. "If you managed to lay hands on me."

"Ah, yes. You're a sorceress, they say. And, I imagine, like all your people, willing to deal death with a crook of your little finger, and no thought to the consequences."

"Have I done so?" Oria asked in her mildest tone. Honey to trap the stinging insect. "It seems to me that I, personally, have done nothing to be treated as the enemy."

"We don't know, do we? Such things are done from behind golden masks and high walls. Perhaps you *were* the one to strike down my husband." Salaya's voice vibrated with rage and her hands shook until she clenched them into fists at her sides. The other women looked askance, pretending not to hear, to be busying themselves with their tasks. But every ear was riveted to the exchange—and if the Destrye were remotely like Bárans, everyone ready to spread the gossip as soon as they left the room. If Oria wanted to establish a fearsome reputation among these people, this would be the time. And yet, something in Salaya's mien spoke profoundly of abject grief. They'd all lost so much.

"I've never struck down any man," she said, willing the Destrye woman to hear the honesty of her words. After all, Oria had only ever killed a woman. "Who was your husband?"

"As if you don't know," Salaya spat.

Oria held up her open palms. "I honestly don't. I am new to your realm and have been ill."

Salaya's mouth turned in disgust. "Yes. Ill and weak. A sad and sorry excuse for a queen. Had Ion lived, he would have succeeded his father and *my* sons would inherit the throne. Strong boys from a real Destrye woman. Now we are to accept you instead." She popped open her fists in a spray of fingers that dismissed the likelihood of such a scenario, adding a word in Destrye that communicated her derision.

This was Prince Ion's widow then. The moment came back to Oria, in horrific detail as if she'd witnessed it from much closer than from atop her high tower. The dragon landing at the edge of Ing's Chasm, snaking its sinuous neck just as Chuffta would, creating a living bridge across. The Trom rider stirring at the wing joints, then walking along its steed's neck over the chasm to the palace side. The Destrye king—Lonen's father—confronting it, then falling to its lethal touch. Ion had been the other man, leaping to defend the king and crumpling also, his sword and strength useless against the Trom's ancient magic.

"I am very sorry," she told Salaya, in all sincerity. "I saw Prince Ion fall. He died bravely, defending King Archimago. But it was not a Báran who killed him; it was one of the Trom. I can only say that it happened very fast. He would not have felt pain."

"Ion would have relished pain!" Salaya hissed, but she'd lost some of her fire. "These Trom, the same who flew on dragons to burn our crops—you also claim they kill with only a touch?"

"Did not your own warriors bring back the tales?"

Two of the women murmured in a far corner and Salaya threw them a glare. Absurdly it pleased Oria to share some of the widow's ire with others. "Warriors," Salaya scoffed. "They tell us what they think we wish to hear. They send us off on a fool's journey to find a new home and then spin stories of fantastic magics, hollow victories, and painless death."

"The Trom are real." Oria took up her mug of tea, now cooled. "And their touch *is* death. Fast, painless, and unstoppable. I'm very sorry for the deaths they dealt your people."

"They kill with a simple touch, you confirm it." Salaya's gaze held a speculative gleam. "And His Highness has declared that none may touch you. Perhaps you are one of these monsters."

Interesting, if convoluted, logic. And yet some truth in it unsettled Oria. No one seemed to be sure where the Trom came from—or the answer lay in the temple texts she'd barely missed being able to access—but they were human-like, if not actually human. Their magic, too, bore some resemblance to what the Báran priests and priestesses used. Her sgath vision had shown their magical presence as a densely powerful black sun, both familiar and not. Some visceral part of her had recognized it. Just as they'd recognized her. The Trom had touched her and it had done nothing beyond making her skin crawl in revulsion. Those matte black eyes, as in the nightmare, had stared into her heart and found a mirroring darkness. *Queen Ponen*, it had called her. *Someday you will call to us and your understanding will deepen.*

Much as she craved answers to the questions that burned at her, she dreaded that such a day might come.

"His Highness makes commands for his own reasons," Oria replied. "I did not kill Prince Ion, nor am I one of the Trom."

Salaya's fingers twitched and she took a half-step forward. "Prove yourself then. I'll touch your skin and find out for myself what sort of poison you ooze."

"You have sons, Salaya," Oria cut into the woman's fugue with words sharp as any blade. "Would you leave them motherless, also?"

Salaya paused, lips trembling then firming, and she swallowed something down. "I… My boys are so young."

It seemed like a non-sequitur, but Oria somehow followed. She nodded. "The children are innocent of all crimes. We owe it to them to bring them up as best we know how. Your sons need you."

"They should have been princes." Salaya sounded almost pleading. She reminded Oria forcefully of her own mother, the labyrinthine drag of grief and helpless anger at events beyond anyone's control.

"They are still princes," Oria said firmly, belatedly realizing this might not be true according to Destrye law—or Lonen's current policy. Though if Lonen wanted her on board with his rule, then he'd have to let her in on discussions and information. She supposed getting actual clothes so she could leave his bedchamber would be the first step. What had Lonen said to her though, back on her rooftop terrace when she first proposed this crazy plan for a marriage of alliance between them? *My older brother left two sons behind when he ascended to the Hall of Warriors. By Destrye law, the crown passes to my father's children first, before going to the next generation. But if I have no sons and Arnon persists in his refusal to be my heir, then Ion's sons would be next in line.* All right then. "They are still princes," she repeated, "and Dru needs all its heroes. Look how much has already turned upside down. Who knows what the future may bring?"

"It's true," Salaya breathed. "You are not yet queen. And not yet with child, I think." Her gaze fell to Oria's midsection, and she made herself stay upright and unflinching, resisting the urge to wrap an arm protectively around her empty womb. She also declined to confirm or deny Salaya's supposition. Soon enough they'd have to confront that she could not bear Lonen any heirs. But that fell beyond much larger and more daunting obstacles. "Then you—" Salaya broke off at someone's approach.

Baeltya entered the room, bearing a basket of supplies, and she paused, raising her brows at Salaya. "Lady Salaya. How encouraging to see you out and about. Young Mago and Kavon will be delighted to see their mother."

If Oria had not been long practiced at keeping an impassive expression, she would have winced at the sweetly couched accusation. As it was, Salaya flushed and ran a trembling hand over her hair. "Have they… my sons have asked for me?"

Baeltya softened. "Yes. Go to them, Salaya. There's no need for you to be here."

Salaya cast Oria a speaking glance. "I am not the worst of your problems. Look to your husband, Báran sorceress. There are others who weave their spells today." Seeming pleased to have scored a point, Salaya stalked out of the room.

~ 6 ~

"Nolan is not joining us, I take it?"

Arnon shook his head, shrugging cheerfully. "He said he had a stop to make and would meet us at the storage silos. He's happy, though, that you're taking stock of the situation here in Arill City. We're both glad to see you out and about."

Lonen had to admit, getting outside and into the bracing air of the forest was doing him good. Buttercup, too, pranced with high spirits, the great warhorse also pleased to be released from the confines of the stable. Even Alby, riding behind, ever loyal and attentive, seemed more relaxed. Much as he didn't care to leave Oria alone, Lonen had yielded to Baeltya's well-couched arguments that his hovering made Oria seem weak and in need of protection. If he wanted her to be accepted as Queen of the Destrye, then he'd have to treat her as he would any Destrye woman. Which had always meant leaving them to their own devices and Arill only knew how women spent their time. He'd certainly paid little attention to what Natly was up to when they were not together.

Mostly he'd been happy enough at her absences, as her presence had been distracting at best and infuriating at worst. He'd never missed her as he'd begun to miss Oria the moment he left his chambers. As if he'd forgotten something critically important, like his iron battle-axe, some part of him kept triggering a minor alarm. Enough so that he kept setting a hand to the worn wooden handle before he remembered that, yes, he did have his favored weapon and that, against all reason, he'd deliberately left his heart behind.

You have to get out of bed sometime. Nolan's voice snickered in his head, echoed by Ion's long-ago taunt, *Don't let a bit of foreign pussy make you think with the little head instead of the big one.*

Oria had been an addicting fantasy from the moment he first saw her, and his obsession with her had only increased over time. He'd even entertained for a while the idea that she had cast a spell on him, to occupy his thoughts so, waking and dreaming. But his connection to her had only deepened since she'd depleted herself of magic. For whatever reason, he loved her with everything in him. More than he loved his own people. A truth he'd never speak aloud, though Arill undoubtedly knew his heart.

Arnon glanced over with an assessing expression. "You look better. Baeltya says that, with continued treatments, you should be back to your robust self soon."

Lonen grunted at that. He did feel better. It had been foolish, in retrospect, not to have called in a junior healer to tend him and Oria sooner. But then, he hadn't been quite right in the head. More like a frenzied wolf, pacing the den to protect its mate and allowing none close enough to aid either of them. Some of it he could put down to fever. The rest…

Back to Oria and his crazed feelings for her. At some point he'd stop questioning them and simply accept that he wasn't at all rational where she was concerned. He'd have to factor that in, like a warrior subject to the red rage might. Every man had his weakness and—no, not that. Oria was not his weakness.

His unreasoning passion. Before her, his life had become a bleak landscape of death, grief, destruction, and toil. Oria brought magic with her.

That could only be good. For him and the Destrye.

"Baeltya says the sorceress is also stronger," Arnon continued in a such a bland tone that Lonen bristled internally.

"Her Highness, Queen Oria?" he asked. "Your sister by marriage, you mean? You could inquire after her health. That would be the civil approach."

"Don't pick a fight with me," Arnon replied mildly. "It's not me who has an issue with your marriage to the Báran princess."

"Then you've decided I'm under no spell?" A flock of ravens took off from the bare branches above, croaking out their scolds and warnings, sifting ice crystals down upon them. Oria would like seeing them, perhaps enjoy the taste of melting snow. He could envision her, pale skin pink with the chill, her copper eyes bright with delight as she tipped her fine-boned face to the sky to catch snowflakes on her tongue.

"Oh, you're under a spell all right, just not one born of Báran magic, I'm thinking." Arnon gave him a rueful smile. "Nolan doesn't recognize a man in love when he sees him."

"And you do?" Lonen retorted, a bit stung and exposed by that.

"I do now," Arnon agreed with good cheer, not at all daunted. "Remember, I watched you with Natly, and there's no comparison. For whatever reasons you've given yourself that you married the—that you married Oria, the primary one is clearly how you feel. For good or ill, it seems we must accept that reality."

"And you think it bodes ill."

"Not for you, no—though Nolan does." Arnon closed one

eye, peering at the dark lace of branches above. "But you and I both know it could mean trouble for Dru. If you're blind to that, then I might have to change to Nolan's view."

"I thought you were the one who warned me against making Natly queen. Would any woman please you, or are you so jealous?" The wounded wolf in him leapt, quick to anger. And the reproving look Arnon shot his way made Lonen immediately sorry for it.

"Natly *would* make a terrible queen," Arnon agreed without rancor. "I stand by that opinion. But this foreign sorceress? She's turned your head in a way Natly never did, no matter the wiles she worked." He held up a hand to forestall his brother's reply. "I'm not saying it's magic. I'm only asking you to listen to yourself. To *think*. Setting all else aside, answer this: will Oria make a good queen for the Destrye?"

"She is a sorceress of great power. We need her to protect us from the Trom. They will return. Surely you do not doubt that. Her brother Yar is king of Bára, worse than his forebears. Oria knows him, knows how to fight him. He wants Dru's resources and won't hesitate to strip us of them—and to strip us to the bone in the process."

Arnon nodded, looking thoughtful. "I don't disagree. In fact, I'm sure you're correct on that. Today will show you where we stand on making it through the rest of winter as long as there are no further incursions. But, Lonen—I say this as your brother and your friend—the sorceress need not be queen to accomplish any of this."

Lonen clamped down on his immediate jerk of protest. Arnon was right. And Oria herself had made the same argument, that she didn't need to be queen in Dru. But she did need to be Queen of the Destrye to shelter the people within her magic—yet another thing that would be difficult to explain. Still, she didn't have to be his only wife to accomplish that. Being brutally honest with himself, Lonen could see how part of his desire to make Oria queen lay in his boyish wish to give her the best, to prove to her that he could. He might not be able to return her to the elegant life she'd lived before, but he could build her towers to live in, make her a garden that would at least thrive in summer. He might be nothing more than a mind-dead barbarian, the furthest thing from the ideal sorcerer-mate who would have lifted her to magical heights, the husband she'd dreamed of, but he could dress her in the finest furs and give into her hands the might and power of ruling the Destrye.

Not honorable thoughts, none of them to his credit. All born of pride and vanity.

But there were honorable reasons, too, not the least of which that Arill Herself had guided his footsteps in this. The goddess had bound him to Oria both in blessing and as retribution for the terrible acts he'd committed in war. Arill meant for Oria to be Queen of the Destrye. He'd vowed as much in the goddess's name and he would not be forsworn.

"As long as I am king," he said, letting his trust in Arill suffuse the renewed vow, "then Oria is my wife and queen. I will not set her aside for any reason."

Arnon sighed. "You always were the stubborn one among us. I told Nolan as much."

"He put you up to this?"

"He wanted me to suggest setting the sorceress aside as queen, yes."

Lonen swore at that, but Arnon reined up and put a steadying hand on Lonen's forearm. "I want you to think about this, and this is only me talking. Forego making Oria queen. Marry Natly instead if you must. Or marry Salaya and make Ion's sons your heirs as would please the people and perhaps Arill Herself. Keep the sorceress as a mistress. None would question that she is your trophy, least of all Salaya, who would likely not want to share your bed regardless."

Lonen gripped his brother's shoulder, looking hard into the younger man's intelligent brown eyes. "Is this what the Destrye have come to? For decades we've worked to shed our past. We are no longer barbarians to abduct women and keep them as trophies. I vowed to Oria to be her husband. Would you have me go back on that, dishonor all we've done to become better men?"

Arnon returned his gaze. "Would you embrace that honor and be dead? Because that's what it will come to. If you do not set aside the sorceress, Nolan will challenge you and you know he is the superior fighter. He'll kill you. Not because he wants to, but because he believes it's best for Dru. Isn't that also honorable?"

When Lonen dropped his hand, shaking his head, Arnon persisted. "He's not wrong and you know it, Lonen. You say this is about honor, but isn't it more about your affection for this woman?"

"It can be both."

"And you can be both right and on the side of honor—and it might still come down to one more of my brothers dead. Dru needs us all. We can't afford to be killing each other. Think about that when you weigh your decision."

"I've already made up my mind."

"Of course you have." Unexpectedly, Arnon grinned, though weariness mixed with the affection in it. "When have you ever *not* been set on your path? I'm asking you to think long and hard about whether this is the right time to be stubborn, the right thing to be stubborn about. Your certainty is a strength. Don't let it be your curse."

"I'll think on it," Lonen conceded, mostly to end the conversation.

"Thank you." They rode on for a bit, the dense trees giving way to brighter light that signaled a clearing ahead. "One more thing for you to weigh," Arnon lowered his voice, glancing at him, back at Alby and his squire, and away again. Lonen braced himself, for the set of his brother's jaw signaled his unhappiness. "Perhaps it hasn't occurred to you, but I am the one who should serve as my brother's second in any duel. And I can't be second to both of you at once."

"Are you saying that you'd choose Nolan's side?" Lonen asked the question evenly and without emotion. Oria would be proud.

"I'm asking you not to make me choose." The weariness crowded out all affection in his voice, and Arnon didn't look at him as he said it.

BY THE TIME Lonen returned to the palace, he too was weary in mind and heart, as well as body. Although he felt better than he had the day before, and it seemed possible that soon a short outing wouldn't exhaust him.

Holding on to hope that everything else would improve proved more daunting.

Despite the depredations of war on the numbers of warriors and the trials of the Trail of New Hope on the rest of the Destrye population, he still had far more mouths to feed than food to put in them. The decimation of the crops in late fall by the Trom and their dragons had done them in. At the current rate of consumption—already strictly rationed—they'd run out of food easily two months before the earliest crops could yield fruit, and that was hoping for a gentle spring. Even if they sent hunting parties further afield, to forests where they hadn't thinned the game beyond the herds' abilities to recover, and grimmer math predicting losses to hunger, disease, and cold, that only bought them maybe another month.

Ironically enough, the reservoirs Arnon and his engineers had constructed held plenty of water to see them through, even keeping in reserve several to irrigate crops through the summer. Heavy snows had fallen early and Arnon had wisely tasked teams of otherwise idle warriors to gather the snow from the fragile rooftops of the hastily built wooden city sprawling around the temple and palace—both relieving the structures of strain and supplementing the water reserves.

But if they were to make it through the winter, they'd have to slaughter the egg-laying poultry and brood livestock. The short-term solution would only leave them worse off the next winter.

Die now or die later, Nolan had commented with a malicious smile. *We'd have done better to perish on the battlefield and have at least taken those cursed Bárans with us.*

Lonen had left his brothers bickering over the math, citing very real fatigue. He hated how Nolan's inquiry after his health sounded like another calculation, this one counting down the days until the duel. The lightweight wreath of hammered golden leaves weighed heavily, and he nearly handed it to Alby along with his outdoor fur cloak on entering the heated palace, remembering even as he lifted his hand to it that his responsibilities could not be shed so easily.

Or perhaps they could. He could abdicate—in Nolan's

favor or in Mago's. Surely kings had done so before him. It might not necessarily be a failure. Wasn't there wisdom in knowing when to retreat? If he dueled with Nolan, he'd almost certainly be defeated, which meant death. Either way he'd lose. And so would Oria and the Destrye.

The only path he could see through the dense forest of decisions was to take advantage of his powerful sorceress wife. They needed her back at full health and magical strength.

Dismissing Alby, he turned his steps, taking the branching passage to the bridge to Arill's Temple rather than hastening back to Oria. There was some kingly discipline. It could be enough to know she would be there, waiting for him when he returned. He'd make it be enough.

And it was time to take his questions to the goddess.

He made his way to the royal family's chapel, the sacred chamber where all their private prayers and rituals were conducted. He'd walked it so many times, his feet knew the way of their own accord—though they'd often dragged when he'd been a boy, his small and sullen rebellion against the boredom of the enforced visits. Back then the corridor had seemed excruciatingly long, the chapel dark and even some-what scary. The carving of Arill over the altar had always reminded him of his mother, who had wielded her disap-pointment and disdain with devastating accuracy.

By the time he reached the age of five, he'd far preferred facing his father's anger or even his brother Ion—older by seven years—gleefully dealing bruises with the flat of his sword than one of his mother's heart-to-heart discussions. She'd had a knack for laying open his failings, gently but ruthlessly exploring his character and suggesting improvements. How a reckless boy might think ahead to the consequences of his actions. How a careless boy might slow down and pay attention to his lessons. That, while the illustrated tales of past deeds might be exciting, the son of a king had better ways to spend his time.

In the quiet of the chapel, Arill's painted visage stared down at him with gray eyes exactly like Queen Vycayla's. Her slight smile seemed both knowing and—while forgiving—also pained that he'd needed forgiveness in the first place.

Arill knew his blackest heart, had borne witness to all the dark deeds he'd done in the name of war and in the name of lust. After the siege at Bára, when he'd returned home an unwilling king and starving victor, he'd repented to Arill, purging himself in Her harshest ceremonies. Something in Her smile, however, always left him feeling some taint remained, the certainty that not only had he never measured up, he likely never would.

Her eyes forever mirrored his mother's disappointed love. Perhaps that was the answer he sought—that he should abdicate in favor of Nolan or Mago. No one had meant for Archimago and Vycayla's carefree third child to govern the Destrye.

Is that Your message, Arill? Should I step down and let my betters rule?

Arill's sad smile spoke of Her grudging approval. Her open palm offering a heavy-headed stalk of grain gave him surcease. And yet... Her other hand held the scythe. The goddess both grew the crops and harvested them. The gleam of the fine-edged blade drew him, always had. He was a warrior, not a farmer.

His had been a battlefield promotion and, now that the battle had ended, he could demote himself again. But the hair prickling on the back of his neck told him the war was not yet over.

Something about Her hands though… There was another image of Arill, one he'd always loved, and She hadn't held the grain and scythe, had She? In that one She'd looked not disappointed, but benevolent. And Her eyes were tawny gold, Her hair fair and fiery.

A scuffling sound startled him enough that he'd half-drawn the battle-axe out of reflex before he caught himself, resheathed it, and turned. *No golems here,* he reminded himself. *Not yet,* the hairs on his neck whispered.

Priest Robson eyed him with disapproval from under silver-white brows, spider-leg long with age. "I took you to be praying, Your Highness. Have Arill's children fallen so far back into the old ways that you come before Her armed as if for battle?"

With some chagrin, he shrugged, the weight of the axe heavy now between his shoulder blades, but the priest's question resonated oddly with his own forebodings. "I've carried it so long, my axe has become another limb. I forget it's there until I reach for it. So perhaps so, Rhiten. Perhaps I am regressed to our barbaric past." *A careless boy. A reckless boy.*

"Is that why you've come here today?" Priest Robson asked, more gently. "It's no feast day, nor a day for regular observance, but neither have you been to pray to Arill since your return to Dru."

"I've been ill," he replied, feeling more than a little defensive. Did everyone want something from him? Of course, he knew the answer to that.

"And so you have. But the spirit requires healing from despair as much as the body does from injury. You've sent for a healer. Why not your spiritual guide, your rhiten?"

He couldn't very well say that it hadn't occurred to him. Or that when it had, it had felt like the lowest of priorities.

Instead he met the priest's keen gaze. "I'm here now."

"Then let us pray."

"Rhiten, I don't really have time to—"

The old man pushed past him and, leaning heavily on his staff, knelt before the altar. He looked over his shoulder with some impatience. "Do you tell Healer Baeltya you have no time for her treatments, to drink her teas? I thought not. Kneel down and clear your mind, boy."

Setting aside the pull of restlessness, the urge to get back to Oria, he obeyed old rules and knelt beside the priest, attempting to clear his mind. The memory came back, vividly bright and clear, of kneeling like this in the temple at Bára, preparing to wed Oria. She'd teased him, copper eyes shining with magic and laughter, telling him he was supposed to be meditating.

"What in Arill does that mean?"

"Like... praying to your goddess. Silently."

"Now what?"

"Keep doing it. And be quiet."

"Why would I keep doing something I already did?"

"You're supposed to be contemplating!"

"Contemplate what? I already made the decision about the step I'm about to take. There's no sense revisiting it."

Like praying to his goddess. Only he'd never much seen the point of that either. The purging rituals, the sacrifices— those made sense and consumed all of his attention with their grueling demands. Strange to look back on that moment, to taste again in his memory that certainty. He had made the decision to wed Oria despite the wide array of reasons not to, and he hadn't needed to revisit it.

Yes, her arguments had made logical sense, once he got past the shock at the audacity of her idea, but that hadn't been why he'd ultimately gone along. Even when he'd questioned his own sanity, even wondered—like his brothers did, he had to admit—what sort of magic she might have used on him, he'd never lost the bone-deep certainty that she was meant to be his wife.

A gift from Arill.

Or a punishment from the goddess.

His, either way. No matter what.

Casting his eyes up at Arill's image, it seemed Her smile held only approval, Her gray eyes alight with challenge.

~ **7** ~

"THIS IS A bath?" Oria gazed at the steaming basin of water—no deeper than the first knuckle of her forefinger and the size of her hand—with some dismay. The pot Baeltya used for tea held more fluid.

The young serving girl with the morning-flower blue eyes twisted her fingers together. "I beg your pardon, my lady, but… yes. The water restrictions—"

"Surely don't apply here," another serving woman interrupted. "Let us bring out one of the queen mother's tubs and fill it. That's what Lady Natly—"

"No." Oria held up a hand, and not only because she didn't want to hear what Natly did or didn't do. That was all she needed to improve her reputation among the Destrye, to prove herself a wastrel as well as the enemy who'd deprived them of their water reserves in the first place. She needed to stop being so thoughtless.

"You're not thoughtless. This is all new to you."

"And you are too generous with me."

"Because I love you. I suggest rolling in hot sand—that cleans my hide nicely."

"Leaving your scales dry and peeling. You'll be in need of oil."

"I am itchy," her Familiar admitted, and she felt another pang for having neglected him.

Time to take more control of her situation. Her hand still in the air, the serving women eyeing her with breath held and faces anxious, she studied their glossy curls, shining with volume and vitality. Surely the palace ladies had ways of washing their hair, if only to keep the vermin out. The very thought of insects breeding in her hair made her skin crawl as if a Trom had touched her.

"I would pick them out for you."

"Ah…Thanks. How about we save that for a last resort?" Out loud, she asked, "How do you all cleanse your hair?"

The ladies exchanged nervous glances. "Us? Or the noble women?" the blue-eyed girl ventured.

"Both. Either, since it seems there's a difference."

The girl gestured to the bowl. "The noble ladies use a cloth and bowl, as such."

"Even to wash their hair?"

She giggled, more nervous than anything. "We do that in spring, traveling to the lakes when they've thawed. Or some women of the outer buildings have been gathering snow and melting it."

"In winter we use powders to soak up the excess oils," another put in, eyeing Oria's hair with some doubt. Even with it knotted up again, she could feel it heavy with the sweats of sleep and sickness. The wiry and curly hair of the Destrye women clearly withstood far more oils than her mass of fine, straight strands. They had no mirrors, it seemed—she recalled Lonen's fascination with hers back in Bára—so she could only imagine how awful she must look. It made no sense to dress her up to dine in the fine clothes and furs being industriously sewn for her, when the person inside the pretty garments stank with filth. How she longed for the steaming baths of Bára.

"Perhaps I should cut my hair short, like Salaya," she suggested, nearly taking a step back when they exclaimed in horror.

"Begging your pardon, my lady," the blue-eyed girl said. "Lady Salaya's hair is shorn out of mourning for her husband's death. If you were to do such a thing…"

Ah. It would appear that she considered Lonen dead. Even though the popular opinion seemed to be that they weren't truly husband and wife. It would be nice if the Destrye would make up their minds about that.

"If you don't do the bowl and cloth method, what *do* you do?"

"The aswae in Arill's Temple," blue eyes replied, ignoring the others, including the senior servant who tried to shush her. "But it's public and all the common women go there. The more refined ladies bathe in private."

"How does it work—what is an aswae?"

"It's a wooden room with benches. And they build up the fire very hot. We rub oil on our hair and skin, then scrape it off again. The sweat from our bodies makes it quite cleansing."

"Sounds delightful."

"You would like that." But she agreed that the prospect of being warm enough to sweat was enticing indeed. "All right. Will you take me there?"

The other serving women looked aghast and fell to muttering among themselves, but blue-eyes nodded, her chin firm. "I will. And I'll tend you myself. Let me find you something to wear."

While Oria waited, she wandered about the chambers, sipping her tea and eavesdropping on the Destrye women as they conversed. From what she could pick out, several seemed to find Oria's proposed visit to the aswae quite scandalous while others shrugged it off.

The helpful serving girl returned with a plain gown of thick material. "It's not a lady's dress," she explained, "but decent for a trip to the aswae, if you don't mind." Oria did not mind a bit. The outing had begun to feel like an adventure—and a welcome respite from the crowding of her sanctuary. Wearing the gown, an additional cloak and her fur slippers, she held up a hand to Chuffta, who glided down from his perch on the ceiling beam, to land on her shoulder. He looped his tail around her throat, more out of affection than anything else, as the thick cloak gave him excellent purchase, and delicately poked his nose at her hair.

"I don't see any vermin," he commented.

Before she could frame a tart reply, the serving girl, eyes wide and shocked, blurted out, "You don't mean to bring your pet!"

Several women fell silent, some shooting glares at the girl, as if to admonish her for impertinence, the others avidly interested. "Yes," Oria replied, finding it easy to remain serene on this one. "Chuffta needs cleansing and oiling, too. And he loves the heat."

"All right," the girl replied, shrugging for the vagaries of crazy noble ladies. "It's not like they'd dare criticize you, anyway."

Not to her face, that was.

The girl led the way out the door and into a corridor. Like all the rooms Oria had seen thus far, the hall was built entirely of wood, long strips of it fitted together along the long sides, arching up from a flat floor, then bending overhead to form a point. The colors shifted in a subtle spectrum from dark to light and back again, like a rainbow of brown. Oria trailed her fingers along it, the texture not like wood or bark at all, but smooth as sueded silk. They must do something to it, to make it feel so fine. Smaller pieces in various shapes and colors made up the flooring, the swirling pattern giving her a curious sense of swaying branches.

Destrye guards that had been outside the doors now followed after, not speaking to her but also not commenting to each other as the serving women might have. Alby had no doubt gone with Lonen, as he always did.

"What is your name?" she asked the girl. None of the serving women had offered their names, although she wasn't sure if they observed some sort of protocol, believed she wouldn't be interested, or had some other reason.

"Pilaryh," she replied without hesitation.

"Why didn't you offer your name earlier?"

"We weren't sure of your customs. Báran ways are strange." She cast a glance at Oria, the blue of her thickly lashed eyes a vivid contrast with her golden skin and burnished dark curls. They were very nearly the same height, which made Pilaryh short for a Destrye.

"Báran custom is that you should call me Oria," she said. No matter that wasn't strictly true. She tired of hearing the deliberate omission of honorifics. Not that she blamed the serving women. They all found themselves in a snarl.

Pilaryh led them over a sort of bridge that Oria vaguely recalled from Lonen's rescue of her from the healing ward at the temple. Tacked-down hides covered large holes cut at regular intervals in the walls. One had come loose, flapping in a chill breeze, so Oria paused, lifting the corner.

"That should be fixed," Pilaryh noted. "In the summer the Bridge of Seofe is open to the warm breezes and the view is quite nice. But this time of year it's too cold."

"May I look anyway?"

Pilaryh cocked her head, giving her a funny look. "I'm

pretty sure you get to do whatever you want, my… Oria." She gestured to the guards. "Remove this hide so the sorceress may look out."

One man stepped up and made short work of it, standing back and holding the hide while Oria stood in the open frame, the chill pouring in. On her shoulder, Chuffta lifted his nose, scenting the breeze. He'd been in and out, taking in the sights, telling her some of what he'd seen, but he had a peculiar perspective at times. And though she loved the cloistered warmth of Lonen's chambers, she'd greatly missed the vistas she'd lived with all her life.

Now it seemed she stood high among branches. Naked of leaves, they twined like black snakes against a gray sky, rattling against each other with thin-boned murmurs. On one side of the bridge, a graceful construction of wood surrounded the largest tree she'd ever seen. It wove in and out, echoing the lines of the branches and limbs. Arill's Temple. At the other end, where they'd come from, an uglier structure squatted. Made of heavy wood, it looked like the fortress the palace was. The warrior counterpart to the elegant, airy goddess.

All along its walls, below the bridge, at the base of the temple and radiating out in every direction, more wooden buildings sprawled. These were not made with any design or the most basic nod to decoration. None seemed to be square. Even the simpler cubes weren't perfectly aligned, and they often branched into triangular wings or sprouted narrow passages. They piled on top of each other, the ceiling of one the apparent floor of another.

A haphazard series of catwalks and ladders allowed people to move among them, which they did. Children with dark curling hair ran shrieking up and down the passages, sometimes leaping from one level to the next, making Oria catch her breath in dismay. They seemed to be partly helping, partly getting into trouble among the adults who worked on the topmost roofs, which sported slanting boards that shunted snow into troughs. The people looked to be gathering it up and giving to others to carry away. To be melted, no doubt, as Pilaryh had mentioned.

Snow and ice. She'd imagined it more beautiful than this. Not grimy and packed down. It didn't look like anything one would want to drink.

"It's prettier when it's fresh. It snowed several days ago and not since. When it's fresh, it looks like sand, drifting and smooth." Chuffta showed her an image of it.

The conglomeration of the Destrye city rose and fell in waves. She could see it as not unlike sand dunes, with a ridge at the distant edge, the buildings there high enough she couldn't see past them, though here and there, breaks between revealed some sort of a deep pit beyond.

"What is that?" She pointed, edging aside for Pilaryh to see.

"The moat." Pilaryh darted her a glance. "You know—full of sharp spikes, to stop the golems."

Ah. Oria stepped back, allowing the guard to reattach the hide, almost sorry that she'd looked. She had not imagined the exuberant, free-ranging Destrye living so crowded together, in such unlovely conditions. What had she expected, though?

"I think they did not always live this way, that may be why you expected otherwise."

That could be, though she hesitated to ask Pilaryh about it. That was how the city looked—like the place a hunted and terrified people might hunker down in to fend off an implacable enemy. Not planned.

The temple itself further confirmed that supposition, with its lovely, arching halls and attention to beauty. Everywhere she looked, some detail adorned the least nook. Leaf and branch designs trailed along lintels. Fruits and sheaves of grain decorated wall panels. Tapestries in vivid colors showed vast meadows and forests of with animals of all types. Branches and twigs from the tree that formed the core of the temple poked through seamlessly, a few still sporting fiery leaves. Here and there, dried leaves scuttled across the wooden floors in the wind of their passage, and Oria recalled how one had fallen onto her in a lazy spiral when she'd first awakened. How the head healer, Talya, had taken it up and set it in a bin.

Picking up one of the dry leaves, she examined it. Larger than her head, it looked unlike the smaller leaves of the trees in her rooftop garden. Rather than a central spine, this one had veins that rayed out like the fingers of a hand to pointed edges. It contained no color—not living green nor the dying oranges. Instead it had gone beige, nearly the color of the dirty snow outside, thinner than the most delicate glass vessel the master forgers of Bára could produce, and it gave off a scent like Baeltya's tea. She brushed her fingers over the sandy surface, producing a sound like she'd touched the finest of scrolls.

"My lady?" Pilaryh asked, a puzzled line between her thick brows.

"It's beautiful," Oria said, a kind of an explanation.

"It's a leaf."

And thus ordinary to a woman who grew up surrounded by these massive trees. They were the counterpoint to that squalid jumble of huts. Holding the leaf, closing her eyes, it seemed Oria could almost sense it out there—a sort of holy silence where the forest breathed softer than sand whisking against glass. A verdant, ancient magic, the quiet unheard heartbeat behind the yammering tangle of wild magic.

She inhaled, taking it in, savoring. It didn't flood her, not like the chaos of the wild magic, nor did it surge in great waves like the sgath below Bára. It infiltrated, another kind of satiation, quenching a deep thirst. Swallowing the unexpected gift, she held it in her heart and belly, keeping it safe.

"Oria?"

Oria opened her eyes to find Pilaryh and the two guardsmen all watching her with suspicion and concern. One guard fingered the hilt of his sword.

"You were standing there meditating for a while. I think you confused them."

"Did you feel it—the forest song?" Abruptly she recalled that delirious moment in the water at the oasis when she'd listened to the enchanting sound of the stars brushing against each other as they danced across the sky. She'd forgotten it mostly, as one did with dreams, checking them off mentally as not real and therefore not worth remembering. But now...

"Would you... like to keep the leaf?" Pilaryh asked gently, the way one would mollify a temperamental child. Or a crazy sorceress.

"Can I?" She did want to keep it. Perhaps work with it to reach for that holy sensation again.

"Well, sure." Pilaryh held out a hand for it. "We normally throw them away." She gestured to a bin in the corner, brimming with leaves that had been crushed as someone tamped them down to make more room. "You can have as many as you like. Or do you want to keep *this* leaf, in particular?"

Oh well, they already thought she was crazy.

"I know I do."

"Which makes you so very clever." She added aloud, "I'd like to keep this one."

Pilaryh stepped to the wall and rang a little brass bell. It made a sound, too, like the stars. Why was everything suddenly reminding her of strange things?

"You're waking up. Now that your body and mind are healing, your natural abilities are resurrecting, searching out the magic to sustain them."

"How could you possibly know that?" She mentally rolled her eyes at Chuffta.

"I am wise in many things," he replied in a smug tone. *"Heed my words and you shall go far, sorceress."*

"I think maybe your mind needs healing." The laughter bubbling up inside felt good. Light, fizzy, and cleansing. Soon she'd be clean all over. Maybe there was hope, as Lonen in his infernally stubborn way always insisted.

A young girl, not old enough to have had her first visit from Sgatha, ran up to Pilaryh, nodded at the instructions and held up her palms reverently for the leaf. Black curls in ringlets spiraled down her back, thickly fringed lashes surrounded crystal clear gray eyes that were enormous with wonder as she stared at Chuffta on Oria's shoulder. Without a word—and without taking her gaze off the derkesthai—she accepted the leaf, bowed and walked back toward the bridge to the palace, moving as carefully as if she carried a precious vessel.

"I would have introduced her to Chuffta," Oria said as they resumed walking.

Pilaryh cast an oblique glance at the Familiar, who snaked his head around the knot of Oria's hair to study her. Probably with a mock fierce glare, knowing him. "It wouldn't … hurt the child?"

"No." Oria nearly laughed, then thought better of it. And of Lonen's warnings. "Not if I command him not to."

"I hear and obey, worthy mistress." Chuffta managed a dead-on imitation of one of the more obsequious Báran council

members.

"Ooh, I like that. Grovel more and maybe you'll earn your dinner."

Chuffta tightened his tail around her throat, only for a moment, but a more subtle move than his usual trick of pulling her hair.

They'd descended far enough that she supposed they must be underground. The light had dimmed and the air smelled moister, earthier. The branches that occasionally surfaced in the corridor ceiling and walls could actually be roots. If roots grew as big around as a Destrye warrior's body. Which, she supposed, they'd have to do, to support those enormous trees.

At a set of wooden doors, banded with gleaming metal, the guards paused and took up stations. Pilaryh knocked on one, and it opened, just enough for Oria to slip through. Pilaryh gestured her in. The heat hit her immediately and she blinked at the relative brightness of the room after the dim corridor. They seemed to be in a sort of antechamber. Shelves lined the walls, divided into cubbies, some with shoes and bundles of clothes. A metal brazier in the middle of the room glowed with hot coals, smelling of herbs that cleared her nose and soothed her mind.

"I like it here!"

Oria put a restraining hand on Chuffta's taloned foot. *"Not yet. Stay with me and let's learn the rules."*

"I was just going to look," he muttered, but he stayed put as Pilaryh barred the door behind them. A stooped older woman craned her neck to peer at Oria, then back at Pilaryh, asking something quietly. Pilaryh replied at some length and the keeper shrugged and nodded. How had that explanation gone? *Here's the king's foreign mistress claiming to be queen. She's probably insane, but she's also a sorceress, has a dangerous pet and doesn't*

know any better. So just play along.

In any case, play along the woman did. She waved Oria to a corner, pointing a crooked finger at Chuffta, then to a bench there, and he obligingly half-glided to the perch. The woman undid Oria's cloak, shaking her head when Oria tried to help, fixing her with a menacing glare from one tawny eye, an unusual shade among Destrye. The other eye appeared to be injured—or missing—the white lines of old scars making a starburst around it. She undressed Oria, deftly folding her clothes and setting them in a cubby, along with her furry slippers. Pilaryh had disappeared into some other corner.

The crone demonstrated that Oria should hold her arms out from her sides, so she did, a little self-conscious at being naked in front of the strange woman. But when the attendant brought over a bowl of golden fluid that had been warming on a shelf under the brazier, dipped her hands in it, Oria stopped her. "Please, don't touch me."

The woman frowned at her and said something. "No," Oria replied. "I'll do it." She reached for it, but the attendant held the bowl away, studying her with that one startling black eye. She nodded to herself, set the bowl back to warm and shuffled off. Returning, she held up her hands, showing Oria she wore hand covers made of leather. She dipped her leather-covered hand in the oil, and stretched it toward Oria. A test then. Holding her breath, Oria held out an arm, bracing for the impact, but the oil smoothed on thick and warm—with no intrusion from the old woman's thoughts or emotions.

She released the breath in relief, then nodded and shared a smile with the woman. Then she lost all caring except for how wonderful it felt.

If the fruit juice had felt like it quenched a core-deep thirst, the oil sated an encompassing one. At first it seemed odd to smear oil over skin that already felt unforgivably filthy, but it sank into her pores with a delightful simmer. With hands surprisingly gentle and deft despite her knotted fingers, the old woman massaged the oil into every inch of Oria's skin, even over her face and between her legs. Instead of feeling intrusive, however, the massage made her feel cared for, loved even.

"Me too?" Chuffta asked, and for a moment she thought he meant being loved, but he held out his wings hopefully. Oria pointed at the bowl, then to her Familiar, making as if to dip her fingers into the oil. The woman snatched it away, however. Before Oria could apologize to Chuffta, the attendant tottered over to him, filled her hands with the oil and began smearing it over his scaly white hide, as if she did it all the time. The woman noted Oria's surprise, winked at her with the good eye, then pointed her chin at a metal teapot simmering on a low flame inside a screened box.

Oria almost demurred, feeling quite full of healing teas, but the crone called out something in Destrye. A naked Pilaryh appeared, her hair now knotted up too, her robust body gleaming with oil. She hastened to pour a cup for Oria, then herself. "It helps bring up the sweat." She smiled over the rim, as natural as if they weren't drinking tea in the nude.

The old woman was working oil into Chuffta's wing membranes with deft grace, and the derkesthai had his eyes half closed in utter pleasure, his thoughts a murmur of delighted commentary. "Will your pet want some tea, too?" Pilaryh asked, all politeness.

"I don't think he sweats," Oria replied gravely.

"Derkesthai glow," Chuffta noted in such a prim tone that she nearly snorted tea. *"But tell Pilaryh thank you for the consideration. And Rachyl that she has a wonderful touch."*

"You caught her name?"

"Mmm."

"Would you thank the attendant for us?" Oria asked Pilaryh, deciding discretion might be better.

"Rachyl will continue to serve you both. At the end, you can gift her to show your appreciation."

Oh wonderful. Oria had nothing to give. Perhaps she could have Lonen send something. Finished with Chuffta, Rachyl took Oria's hand again and held out the other for Chuffta. He didn't usually go to strangers, but he hopped up onto her wrist, carefully wrapping his talons around the old bones so as not to pierce her skin, raising his tail for balance. She grinned at him, then at Oria, a smile missing several teeth, and said something.

"What did she say?"

Pilaryh shook her head. "Something in her tongue. Arill only knows."

"She's not Destrye?"

"Not even a bit, but she's been here forever. This way for the aswae."

Pilaryh opened another door and Oria, Rachyl leading her by the hand still, entered yet another room. Both hotter and dimmer, this one seemed to be lit only by bloodred coals gleaming in metal grates positioned around the room. About a dozen women, all naked, lounged around on benches.

All of them stared at Oria.

Pilaryh seemed not to notice, finding an empty tier of three benches attached to the wall. "Start at the top. If you feel too hot, move down to a lower one. But try to resist. Just keep sweating."

At least lying down, Oria felt less conspicuous. Chuffta arranged himself perilously close to a brazier of coals, belly up and wings spread to their fullest extent, sighing happily. Oria tried to emulate his ease, stretching herself on the topmost bench. She was already sweating profusely, her perspiration mixing with the oil and sliding across her skin. It felt like the hottest afternoon in Bára, without the sun. There, however, they'd never deliberately tried to be hot. Everything had been about cooling—the ices, juices, fruits, shades, and fans.

In this, too, then, the Destrye were opposite. But as the heat penetrated her bones, she felt warm for the first time in what seemed like ages. Rachyl had been tending other women, moving about in the shadows. Oria hadn't really been watching. She returned to Oria, gesturing her to stand again. Working swiftly, she took what looked like a wooden knife, scraping it over Oria's skin, then wiping the dull blade and tossing the refuse onto the coals where it hissed, sending up a smoke that smelled of dark spices and a roasted scent she only then identified. Human skin. Oh joy.

"Humans don't smell so bad once you get used to them," Chuffta's snotty comment lost something in the blur of contentment.

Other attendants worked, too, or some women tended each other, some scraping as Rachyl did for her; others rubbing on oil and massaging. Sure enough, once Rachyl finished scraping every crevice on Oria's body, including behind her ears and the bottoms of her feet, she slathered on more oil and waved for her to lie down again. Rachyl set to work performing the same service for Chuffta, who predictably loved every moment. Oria had long oiled his hide to keep it supple in the desert heat, but it had never occurred to her to scrape it this way. Maybe she could get one of those wooden knives and learn to do that for him.

"Or we could just come here. Every. Day."

She chuckled at that, but tended to agree. The aswae felt wonderful. After a while, Rachyl returned, this time with a cup of fresh water. Oria sipped it as Rachyl scraped her, no longer minding the smell of old skin burning on the coals. She imagined it as all the filth she'd accumulated and it seemed fitting to burn it. Old pains and sorrows, burnt and turned to smoke.

This time, Rachyl took her empty cup and had Oria sit on a lower bench. She took Oria's long hair down and, tugging Oria's head back, poured hot oil through it. The sensation melted through her, leaving utter lassitude behind. This time, when she lay down, her hair once again reknotted, she fell into a deep sleep, free of dreams.

When Rachyl woke her, fewer women occupied the chamber. During the time they'd been in there, women had occasionally left through a second door, and Rachyl, after a final scraping, took her and Chuffta out that door. This room was brighter and almost startlingly cool. Women chatted in louder tones, sliding her glances and conferring as they rubbed themselves and each other down with rough-looking cloths. Rachyl took up a metal flask with a curious attachment and sprayed Oria with a liquid so cool and stinging that her nipples instantly hardened and she squealed—making several of the women laugh.

"It's always startling the first time," Pilaryh said, appearing at her elbow, dark nipples tight with a similar response. "It's like… I don't know the Common Tongue word, like wine, only different. It closes up the pores again."

Rachyl cackled, said something in her tongue which, now that Oria paid more attention, was clearly not Destyre, and sprayed her back, following with the cloth that was rough indeed. Then she applied a lighter oil that smelled of the same spices but absorbed into the skin. Oria herself rubbed down Chuffta, skipping the alcohol spray as it probably wasn't good for him, but using some of the same finishing oil.

Finally, Rachyl sat Oria on a bench with a high back that had divots to rest her neck in. Rachyl unknotted Oria's hair and combed it out, the wooden teeth gliding easily through the thick oil. Oria cracked open her lids at the murmurs, to discover a ring of Destrye women watching. They spoke amongst each other, Pilaryh with them.

She caught Oria watching. "No one has seen hair like yours, like fire," she explained. "They want me to ask, if it won't cause offense. Are all Báran women colored so—or only the sorceresses?"

As her hair had to be nearly black with dirt and oil, she couldn't imagine how they could even tell. "Our hair tends to be much lighter than yours, but not always my color," she replied, closing her eyes and resigning herself to the interrogation. "Ask whatever you like. If I don't want to answer, I won't."

"Your skin, is everyone so fair?"

"Pretty much, yes." Rachyl poured some kind of grit into her hair, massaging it into her scalp. It actually felt good, in an odd way. Stimulating and refreshing after the lulling oils.

"Your nipples are pink," Pilaryh pointed out, and Oria cracked an eye open again.

"Yours are brown," she replied, resisting the urge to cover her breasts. Pilaryh translated for the ladies, who started giggling, cupping their breasts and showing each other. All of them were more endowed than Oria, much in keeping with their larger frames and robust musculature. They had wider hips and voluptuous thighs. One was heavily pregnant, her breasts large and belly swollen. Oria felt like a wraith compared to them. *Wan.*

"It's easy for us to understand now," Pilaryh said, a wistful sound in her voice, "why King Lonen is so obsessed with you. You are the most beautiful woman any of us have ever seen. Perhaps you are the most beautiful woman in the entire world."

Oria nearly choked on that, though maybe that was the powder Rachyl seemed to be dusting through her hair, then brushing out into clouds. "Surely not," she replied. "I'm nothing special. I'm just exotic to you. I would love to have hips and breasts like all of you do." These women looked built to bear children easily and often. Even if Oria could find a way to get with Lonen's child, it seemed impossible that her body could swell to carry such a burden.

Rachyl misted some of the spray onto her hair, then gestured for her to sit up again, draping Oria's hair over her shoulder in a long fall. Impossibly it gleamed brighter than ever, nearly glowing with a healthy sheen. Oria smoothed it, giving Pilaryh a grateful smile. "It worked!"

Pilaryh nodded knowingly. "King Lonen will be most pleased." She patted her own flat belly. "And soon you will swell with his heirs, perhaps even starting one tonight, lovely as you look."

If only it were so simple.

~ 8 ~

L ONEN COULDN'T VOUCH that spiritual healing did anything real. Nothing like what Baeltya did, removing pain and reenergizing his body. But he did feel as if he'd shed his despair. He still wasn't certain of the best decision as far as remaining King of the Destrye. But he also didn't feel that bone-deep weariness just contemplating the choices.

And returning to his rooms, seeing Oria, felt more like a delight to anticipate, rather than fleeing to the comfort of her company to hide himself away.

The guards outside his chamber doors bowed to him. As he strode into the outer chamber, however, he would have doubted that Oria was within if they hadn't said so. The teeming hordes of ladies, maids, and seamstresses who'd driven him out to begin with had all apparently fled. The rooms had been neatened, too, with ashes carried away from the fireplaces, and fresh fires burning, the wood furniture gleaming and furs fluffed.

He supposed they had let it get a bit stale.

"Oria?" he called out, doffing his indoor cloak, tossing aside his wreath of office, and unsheathing his axe to set by the bedroom door. As he entered the room, she rose from her accustomed place by the fire, a lovely flush on her high cheekbones.

"Sorry—I must have dozed off. One day I won't fall asleep at the least opportunity. I went to the aswae and talk about relaxing. It was so warm and they put oil on you—have you done it?—it's so purging and—what? What's wrong?"

He'd been staring. At least he hadn't let his mouth actually fall open, though his tongue felt unaccountably dry. "Oria," he breathed. "You look gorgeous. I mean, you're always beautiful, but—"

She laughed, interrupting the tumble of incoherent praise. Then she stepped out from behind the pair of chairs, held out the skirt of her crimson velvet gown, and twirled. "Isn't it wonderful? I don't know how they knew to make it red— maybe from the rags of my robes—but it's perfect, and I feel almost like myself again."

She spun again, the full skirts belling out, emphasizing her narrow waist and the elegant fullness of her breasts. The high neckline was trimmed with white fur, framing her delicate jaw, and the long, tight sleeves ended in similar cuffs, with long fringes of fur that trailed over her slim fingers. Her hair hung loose and perfectly straight down her back, nearly to her bottom, not billowing in a cloud as it sometimes had in the dryness of Bára, but in a liquid fall as perfectly shining as a newly forged sword.

"And look!" she was saying. With a bright and saucy smile, she picked up a pair of matching velvet gloves from the table between the chairs, which also held a carafe of wine and two mugs. She drew on the gloves and held them up. "I can touch people without worrying about it."

She moved to him with something of her old restless energy, that impetuous grace she'd lavished on every movement back in Bára, and framed his face in her hands, brushing her thumbs over his cheeks, smoothing his beard. Her copper eyes, wide and gleaming, full of light, seemed to glow with her pleasure. "I can't feel, but at least I can touch," she added, her voice throaty.

He encircled her waist with his hands, brutally aware of the swell of her hips below his fingers, the narrow path of her ribcage that begged him to slide his hands up and cup her lovely breasts, tease her nipples until that teasing pretty mouth begged him both to stop and for more. His cock hardened with almost painful ferocity, his darker nature seething to toss her on the bed and throw up her skirts, plundering her until they both wept with exhaustion.

Oria narrowed her eyes slightly. "What are you thinking? You haven't said a word since your astonished observation that I look good."

"Gorgeous," he reminded her quietly. "I said you're gorgeous. And you smell of qinn."

"They put all sorts of stuff on me. I'm not sure which that was."

He knew. Natly—well, all of the Destrye women—used the spice in their soap and oils. It smelled to him of home and comfort. And it did crazy things to his brain to scent it on Oria.

Clearing his throat, he added, "They made the gown red because I told them to. All of your state garments will be red, unless you request otherwise."

She blinked long and slow, considering closing of her eyes. Her lashes were copper, too, and long, but rarely showed until she lowered her lids like that, and then they stood out against the faint scatter of freckles on her cheeks, an almost invisible constellation of fawn stars. Then the full sun of her eyes bored into his again. "Why?"

"A sorceress should have her robes, no matter the material. I have no silk to give you, but you wouldn't be warm enough anyway."

"True," she murmured. "Thank you, Lonen." Her gaze dropped to his mouth. "I wish I could kiss you."

He nearly groaned at that. 'Wishing' didn't come close to how he felt about it. "We'll find a way."

She didn't smile, exactly, but her eyes danced with amusement. "You always do, my Destrye warrior."

Which only reminded him. He let her go and stepped back with a massive effort of will. "Shall we have a glass of wine? There's time before we eat."

"Yes. And you can tell me what's preying on your mind. How was the excursion with your brothers?" She poured him a mug of warmed wine and handed it to him, cupping her own in her gloved hands. "Also, you might change clothes."

He took a swig of wine and set the mug aside. "I no doubt smell of Buttercup, who says hello, by the way." He'd meant to tease her about her attachment to the warhorse, but she looked pleased, as if the steed really had sent a message. "Where is Chuffta, by the way?"

"Stretching his wings. The aswae made him feel frisky, so he's exploring. He'll be back to accompany me to dinner. Enough stalling—what has you worried?"

"What doesn't have me worried?" he shot back. But he told her about the state of Dru as he shucked the day's clothes, found the washing bowl and sponged himself clean of the worst of the day's sweat, then pulled on the clean clothes Alby had left out for him.

Oria listened gravely, asking questions here and there. Finally, she gave him a considering look. "All of this is serious news, but none of it is new. You knew all of this when you left this morning. Before you left to confront me in Bára, in truth."

"I didn't know the exact extent of it," he argued, knowing

as he said it that it wasn't the full truth. He *had* known. Somehow hearing the dire facts recited by his older brother, all of them laid squarely at his feet as if he'd created the situation from his utter carelessness as king, made it all that much more painful. He reached for the wreath of metal leaves, realizing he'd left it in the other room. Some king, forgetting his crown.

Then Oria was in front of him, a staying hand on his arm. "Talk to me, Lonen." Her lush mouth curved in a sly smile. "We're in this together."

He shook his head, laughing under his breath at her ways, then indulged himself by sliding a hand through the sheet of her hair. The ladies had oiled it—probably the source of the qinn, then—which gave it that heavy, silky feel. She gazed up at him, her face so magically lovely that he hesitated to say anything that might dim her regard for him.

"You can't say anything that will make me think less of you," she said softly.

"Reading my thoughts, sorceress?" The prospect, which had once made him uneasy at best, strangely heartened him.

She looked thoughtful. "Not the way I used to, but... some? Maybe. I felt something today, something in the trees..." She shook it off, her hair sliding thick through his fingers. "Never mind that. Tell me what has you so churned up."

"I think," he said slowly, searching for a way to articulate his turbulent thoughts. "Maybe I should abdicate to Nolan. Or to Mago, with Nolan as regent."

"Because of me?" She asked it evenly enough, but he scowled at her.

"No. Because of me. Because I'm ... I'm not a good king, Oria. I was never meant to be one. The Destrye deserve a good king. Not me. I'm careless, undisciplined, reckless, my head always in the canopy."

She tilted her head, considering. Then shrugged. "I don't know this man you're speaking of."

"I'm trying to explain that this is who I am. You haven't known me long, but I—"

"Oh nonsense!" She broke in and broke away, once again that imperious princess who'd laid out his options with ruthless clarity while the quiet towers of Bára stood sentry around them. "I'd venture that I know you better than anyone else, just as you know me. We've crossed the desert together, nearly drowned in the bore tides together, fought back to back, saved each other's lives and listened to each other's deepest fears when things seemed bleakest. You have flaws, Lonen—I won't deny that. You're ridiculously stubborn, won't leave well enough alone. That you remain so optimistic in the face of impossible odds never ceases to amaze me."

"So you've mentioned," he said drily. "And the point is that I'm not feeling that now. I'm not sure… Oria, I might not be up to the task."

"All right then," she said, pouring them both more wine, then clinking her mug against his with a sunny smile he could see right through. "Back to the oasis then? Or to one of Bára's sister-cities? It might not be so bad crossing the desert this time, if we actually take some water and food along."

"That's not what I—"

She set down her mug, threw up her hands, and began pacing. "Oh, you mean stay here? What a great idea. You can let Nolan lord it over you for the rest of your days that he got you to knuckle under and admit he's the better ruler. That will be fun."

The image made him want to growl. "I never said he's the better ruler."

"That's *exactly* what you're saying," she snapped back, skirts whirling out as she reached the wall and spun to pace in the other direction. "Whether you step down for him to be king or regent, it would be an admission that you think he's the better man."

"Maybe he is the better ruler!"

"Fine." She shrugged elaborately, like it didn't matter a whit to her. It rankled a surprising amount.

"That's it? No sage and wifely advice to offer?"

She paused, giving him a long look. "My advice? I think, Destrye, that it was easier for me. I had no doubt that Yar would be a terrible king. My potential inadequacies as queen blew away like so much sand in the face of what his rule would mean, for both Bára and Dru. I don't know Nolan. I barely recall him from when he rescued us. Certainly I owe him my life, but other than that, he's a cipher to me. I'm very interested to take his measure tonight. I *do* know you—and you're none of those things you cited. You are canny, wise, deliberate, noble. Even from the beginning you've never been anything but careful with me. You act decisively, yes, but never recklessly, with the possible exception of when you decided to sacrifice yourself fighting an army of golems to save my life."

"I visited Arill's Temple just now, and wondered once again if She sent you to me as a blessing or a punishment," he said in a wry tone.

She beamed with impish glee. "Can't I be both?"

He strode to her, catching her by the hips. "You are both."

She sobered, her gaze intent on his. "And you are King of the Destrye. Accident or challenge from your goddess, it doesn't matter. You don't need to think about if you're good enough to be king, because you *are* king. More—you're the best warrior I've ever seen and your people need a warrior to lead them. You and I both know the war is far from over."

"Yes," he agreed with regret. "Which Nolan doesn't see."

"Maybe he can't. He missed so much. But you see and you know. If you need to worry about something, worry about being the best king you can be. The best man you can be. Though you're already the best there is, to my mind."

"In all the world?" he teased, to cover how much that touched him.

"Well, I don't know. I haven't seen all the world. Once the war is finally over, maybe you can show me."

When the war is finally over. "Do you think we can truly end this conflict and find peace for our people?"

Her smile dimmed and she regarded him seriously. "I think we have to. Or die trying."

Her words riffed over him with premonition. "It could come to that. If Nolan challenges me, I could lose. It would mean my death."

"Then if it comes to that, we'll have to make sure you win."

~ 9 ~

THEY'RE ONLY PEOPLE, Oria chanted to herself as they progressed down to the formal dining hall. *Only people.* But she clung gratefully to Lonen's muscled forearm beneath her gloved hand. Chuffta's tail spiraled down her arm over the crimson velvet, a perfect match to the white fur trim. His iridescent scales often reminded her of a series of bracelets, but against the Destrye gown, his coiled tail looked more like jewelry than ever.

They'd make an exotic sight for the Destrye court. Talking with the women in the aswae had bolstered her confidence considerably. A good thing, as she'd been in a stronger place to give Lonen the pep talk. He moved with more of his usual swagger, his bold masculine exuberance wafting around her.

Now if she could hold up her end of things.

"You will. These Destrye barbarians will be dazzled by their Báran sorceress queen."

"Now you sound like Lonen."

Chuffta mentally preened. *"I have plenty of fire, too, if we need it."*

She stifled a giggle. *"Let's try not to burn anyone."*

"I said if," he replied in wounded tone.

The conversation had distracted her long enough to get them down a flight of stairs. She hadn't been this way before—

at least, not while conscious. The lower parts of the palace had no windows, not even the hide-covered ones of the upper levels. And the walls seemed to be built entirely of enormous logs. Not the occasionally surfacing living branches of Arill's Temple, but cut trunks of whole trees—three or four of the massive things forming one wall to the ceiling. But surely, they weren't—

"Originally, the palace was a fortification," Lonen murmured to her, following her gaze. "Before the Destrye learned to take only dying trees and deadfall, we cleared parts of the forest for farming. We used the felled trees to build several forts, in various quadrants of Dru."

"Then the walls are…?" she asked faintly, unwilling to sound silly by suggesting the ridiculous.

"Are as thick as each log is tall, yes. No windows. Only a series of doors and portals. This part of the palace, at least, is virtually impregnable."

"I'm amazed the golems could get to you at all."

He looked thoughtful, gaze roaming the walls up to the ceiling beams—made of trees a quarter of the size, but still enormous. "Holing up in here is pretty much the only thing that saved us," he agreed. "But we can't fit all of Dru into the forts. Plus, it did us little good to save ourselves while your— while the golems stole all of our water and slaughtered our livestock. The Destrye used to be much more scattered throughout Dru—lots of small communities and farms. As they were overrun, people came here, or to the other forts. When you see it… Well, the city around the palace and temple are nothing so beautiful as the towers of Bára."

I think they did not always live this way, Chuffta had observed and she winced for both the truth of that and the apology in Lonen's voice. *"You were right,"* she told her Familiar.

"Yes," he replied, but for once did not sound pleased about it.

They didn't enter the grand hall so much as make their way to that end of the enormous fort. It differed from the part they'd passed through in that it had fewer subdivisions. Otherwise, the massive tree trunks dominated the room, dwarfing even the high table built onto a raised platform at one end.

The roomful of people—along with those at the high table—rose to their feet as they entered. Arnon she recognized from the council chambers at Bára, when their respective peoples had negotiated their all-too-temporary truce. She might have recognized him anyway, as he looked like a younger, leaner, and more relaxed Lonen. To his right stood Salaya, her fine-featured face set off by her short hair, her expression clear and remote. She stared off into the distance, perhaps thinking of days when her husband might have sat beside her.

For all that Salaya had been unpleasant, Oria felt for her. She couldn't imagine facing a formal dinner like this with her late husband's family. Too much to endure on top of the grief. Oria would have sent her a commiserating smile, but Salaya never looked her way.

The man to Arnon's left, on the other side of the empty chair between them, she would have guessed to be a relation, but not Lonen's elder brother. He had to be Nolan, though—cleaned up—as he looked nothing like what she recalled from her brief glimpse of the grizzled, travel-worn man in the forest before she'd passed out.

He had a hard face, his dark beard trimmed ruthlessly short, and his eyes such a sharp blue that the color showed clear across the room like the noonday sun through stained glass. A beautiful Destrye woman stood to his left, her black hair in elaborately piled swirls, studded with metallic bands and glittering jewels. She stared at Oria, lustrous dark eyes full of hatred, until she wrenched her gaze away to smile at Lonen, her full mouth pouting seductively. Her clinging gown revealed her voluptuous curves as she seemed to pose with both studied indolence and sensual grace.

Natly. Lonen's former betrothed. Oria knew her face well, from glimpses into his mind when her abilities worked with such keen activity that she picked these things up without meaning to. Which meant that, even worse, she had images in her head of Natly naked, writhing with sexual abandon in the very bed Oria now slept in, those luscious lips closing around—

Oria shook her head abruptly to clear her mind of the image, suddenly aware she dug her gloved fingers into Lonen's arm. And that he'd covered her hand with his, enfolding it tightly in reassurance.

"Brothers," he said, not pausing in the acknowledgment. "I see you've miscounted—there's one chair where there should be two."

"Your Highness." Nolan stared at her as he spoke. "Surely you don't mean to seat your—"

Lonen went deathly still, the rest of room as uncannily silent. She almost imagined ears growing longer to better hear. "This dinner was your idea, Nolan," he said, as quiet as a snake's hiss. "Consider carefully the steps and words you choose."

"Or what?" Nolan's blue eyes glittered. "Will you call insult?"

"If necessary," Lonen replied easily.

Arnon looked as alarmed as Oria felt. He pointed to the

people to his right, making them shift down, an annoyed warrior at the end leaving to find another seat. "Your Highness, you've yet to properly introduce me to your wife," he said, adding a smile that looked a bit too much like a grimace, but still there. He gestured to the now-empty chair he'd been occupying. "Would you care to sit, sorceress, and dine with us?"

Lonen still vibrated with tension, so Oria took the situation in hand. "Thank you. I'd be most pleased. Lonen, would you perform the introductions?"

Some of that got through to him, because he glanced down at her, gray gaze wary, but not flinty. "Oria, love, meet my younger brother, Prince Arnon."

She ignored the reactions of the others to his endearment—one she'd passed off as meaningless initially, but it appeared to carry even more impact than she'd come to believe—and inclined her head. "A pleasure to meet you, Prince Arnon."

Arnon's smile warmed. "We encountered each other glancingly … in the past, sorceress, but it is truly enchanting to get a chance to know you better. Welcome to Dru. We know you traveled great distances and suffered harrowing trials to help the Destrye in our hour of need."

Lonen's bemusement wafted over her, but she focused on Nolan, whose expression had decidedly soured at Arnon's speech.

"And Prince Nolan," she said, taking the initiative and emphasizing his title ever so slightly, "I have not had the opportunity to thank you for saving my lord husband's life. Please accept my gratitude for your timely intervention."

Nolan's mouth thinned. "You thank me for his life and not yours, sorceress?" What had sounded like an honorific from

Arnon's mouth became an epithet on his brother's tongue, but Oria smiled with all the calm tranquility she'd learned to muster in the face of priestesses far more toxic than this Destrye.

"My life is my own," she answered, pleasantly enough but letting him hear the steel beneath. "It was never yours to give or withhold."

He gazed back at her, not frowning, but sorting through her words. "And your loyalty, sorceress—who owns that?"

Lonen stirred. "Is this a dinner or an inquisition?"

"The question is easy enough for me to answer, love, even if we haven't even been served wine yet." She smiled up at her husband, at his surprise that she returned the endearment and how much that obviously pleased him, then allowed her smile to sharpen as she returned her focus to Nolan. *It's better if they fear reprisals from you.* "I am pledged by binding vows to my husband, Lonen, King of the Destrye—where his loyalty goes, mine follows. His friends are mine. His enemies? Also mine."

"Is that a threat, sorceress?" Nolan asked on a queer intake of breath, a waft of old fear in the air. He'd been on the battlefield at Bára and thus witnessed the mighty—and showy—battle magics of the priests. And he'd nearly died there. No doubt he suffered night terrors, too, as Lonen still did, from the things they'd witnessed. She misliked playing on those wounds, but she'd spoken true: her loyalty lay with Lonen. Or rather, with what was right and true, though she hadn't been able to think of a way to say that without sounding naïve. Fortunately, she and Lonen agreed on what those things were.

She hoped. It didn't bear thinking what she might do if they diverged on that.

"A threat?" she echoed with a bemused smile. "How could

that be, if we are among friends?"

Lonen didn't stir, but his amusement—and a hint of annoyance—filtered from him. "Let us sit," he declared, holding the chair Arnon had vacated for Oria, giving her an opaque look from eyes gone to granite.

"I thought it was funny."

"Thank you."

"But my people have a saying: if you singe the wolf's tail, be ready for his teeth to follow."

"Derkesthai like to battle wolves? Seems… unnatural."

He sniffed mentally. *"It's true that it's unfair. They stand no chance against us. But it can be a fun game. For younglings."*

She folded in the smile at that and stroked his tail, beyond glad to have him with her in this.

"Really, should there be animals at the table?" Natly's question pierced the general shuffling of everyone reseating themselves. She possessed a voice as lush and sultry as her figure, but the querulous undertone made Oria want to wince. "After all," Natly continued, "the Destrye no longer allow hounds and fowl to pick at our table leavings. We don't behave like *barbarians*."

"At least, not in the last week," Arnon quipped. "The journey from brute to civilized man seems fraught with pitfalls and backsliding. Back in the day, allowing women at the table was considered the height of weakness."

Oria, at last gratefully sipping the wine a servant poured, nearly choked on it. Her gaze flew to Arnon who leaned around her to send his verbal sally to Natly. He gave her a twitch of a smile, which broadened when Natly made a noise between a shriek and a growl.

"*She* is a woman, too!" Natly stabbed a finger at Oria that flashed with a long, pointed, and painted bejeweled nail.

"This 'she' you refer to is my wife and queen." Lonen's voice, on the other hand, was pure growl. "You will show—"

"That is a matter of debate and—" Nolan spoke over him, then broke off when Lonen spun on him, nearly nose to nose.

"Respect. You will all show respect and behave like adults, not children, before *our people*, for at least the span of time it takes to eat a meal. Our father would expect that much of us." He leaned around his brother. "That includes you, Natly, though you are not, I might point out, a member of this family."

"I wondered when you'd acknowledge me," she pouted.

"I don't even know why you're here."

"How can you say that, after what we've been together?"

"I spoke to you about this, Natly, at length. That was meant to be the end of things."

He had? When had that happened? Lonen had mentioned nothing about it to Oria. Though she supposed that wasn't an easy tidbit to drop into conversation. And his personal business. She didn't envy him that confrontation.

"You don't get to just tell me things are done," Natly gritted out.

"I'm king," Lonen said simply and turned back to Oria, dismissing his former betrothed with studied disinterest. Waving away a servant who sought to serve Oria from a platter of meat, he signaled to another who brought a special plate just for her. A large bowl of grains in a simmering broth, loaded with vegetables and graced by a puff pastry made golden with the Destrye butterfat, it made her mouth water and her stomach leap with interest.

"Thank you," she whispered to Lonen, enjoying the way his silvery eyes lingered on her lips. He smiled at her.

"Scary sorceress," he murmured, gaze glinting with pure

humor.

"Lady Natly is here as my guest," Nolan cut into the moment.

"How nice for you." Lonen's eyes went flat again, his voice all polite boredom.

"It seemed insulting not to include her," Nolan continued. "To simply let her languish. She might not be actual family, but she's as near to it as any might be. Some might say more so than others at this table."

Beside her, Arnon made a quiet choking noise, but Lonen methodically cut his steak, forking up neat bites. "I seem to recall you firmly rebuffing Natly's attempts at becoming 'part of the family,' brother. Let's see—that was after Ion declined her offer in favor of Salaya's fair hand—" he nodded to Salaya, who still stared into the middle distance, not eating "—but before she moved on to me."

"You seemed happy enough to savor the rewards settling on you," Nolan retorted. "I recall you extensively savoring Natly's many charms before we left to destroy the Báran predators, and I understand you continued to lead Natly on after you returned, promising her that you and she would marry. You must address the question of the honor you owe her. Our father would expect that much of us." He bit out that last, looking tremendously pleased with himself.

Lonen heaved a sigh, then looked at Natly, who continued to sulk, though it seemed her eyes glittered with a kind of excitement at the attention as she looked past him at Oria. It made Oria feel oddly old and weary—especially odd given that Natly was likely older than she. But the Destrye woman did have a legitimate grievance, as she would have married Lonen had Oria not maneuvered him into a marriage of state with her. She couldn't blame Natly for being hurt and angry, particularly at losing a man like Lonen. Oria needed to keep that in mind—that she had what Natly had wanted, had been promised, and lost through unfair means—and keep in her heart compassion for his jilted fiancée. In Natly's place, she would likely not behave well.

Never mind that the bickering felt juvenile at this point. Being honest with herself, she completely reneged on her initial offer for Lonen to keep his former fiancée as a lover, or even install her as Queen of the Destrye while Oria remained in Bára. No one need know about that ill-advised idea. It took her aback at the ferocity of her own emotions on imagining such a situation—to the point that she'd fight tooth and nail to keep Natly's jeweled nails off Lonen.

"Or with fire," Chuffta suggested. *"Burn all her hair off."*

Oria stifled a snort of laughter. *"Don't like her, do you?"*

"'Animals at the table.' I'll show her what real *claws can do."*

She concentrated on eating the truly excellent meal, the grains having soaked up the rich broth so they almost melted in her mouth. Baeltya had outdone herself in instructions, if not actual cooking. Lonen, Nolan, and Natly were arguing in hushed voices, though the harsh cadences came through clearly enough. Destrye at the nearby tables, both men and women, ate in silence, doing their best to overhear the discussion, no doubt.

In Bára, the people would be equally eager for juicy tidbits to feed the gossip mill, but the royal family would never eat in public thus. Of course, for her family, eating had meant doffing the eyeless, mouthless golden masks of their office, something done only in privacy. With a pang of nostalgia, she missed those formal, elegant occasions. The ritual of removing their masks and setting them on the tiles beside their plates, made for that purpose. The relaxed intimacy of those meals.

"I miss Bára, too. Your rooftop terrace."

"The sunshine and the view."

The voices beside her grew in volume and intensity, and she felt Lonen growing commensurately angrier. A passionate, emotive people, the Destrye. Just as well she had her portals so locked down that she didn't get much of it. Mostly she experienced the edges of Lonen's dark and brooding anger, a familiar river that ran deep in him, only occasionally rising to the surface.

"They'll come to blows if we don't stop them," Arnon commented in her ear, strangely cheerful, considering the circumstances.

She'd kind of forgotten about him. "The duel?"

He gave her an odd look, pursing his lips. "Talked to you about that, did he? But that's an interesting point. Not the challenge. Not yet, anyway. I meant Lonen and Natly. Though perhaps we shouldn't try to stop them. A good knock-down, drag-out would serve as a fine pressure release and distraction from Nolan badgering you. Or making any hasty challenges."

She swallowed, glad that eating reminded her not to gape in surprise. "Lonen and Natly…might physically fight…at a formal dinner?"

Arnon grinned crookedly and curled his fingers, making a swiping motion. "Those nails aren't just for pretty. She's like a tree cat with them. Left her mark on more than one warrior hereabouts."

Oria and her brothers had squabbled plenty, but they'd never gotten physical. That would have been a grave lapse in *hwil*, even for a youngling, and if she could've borne even the slightest touch. Of course, her brothers had delighted in laying magical traps for each other. And she'd been too fragile for any such tussling, watching mostly from afar. Forever outside the inner circle.

"It hardly seems appropriate," she murmured to Arnon, "for my husband, the king, to publicly quarrel with his former fiancée." Not only because it put her on the outer edges, yet again.

Arnon stroked his beard thoughtfully. "You're not just for pretty, either, are you? I suspect this is exactly what Natly hopes for. What are you going to do about it?"

"Me?"

"No one else is going to." Arnon dug into his steak with relish, chewing ostentatiously.

"Meaning you won't."

"I'm not the one who's being tested tonight."

She sat back abruptly, Chuffta spreading his wings slightly to rebalance, grumbling at her. "This... scenario is for my sake."

"Lonen always did get easily sucked into Nolan's taunting. And yes, that's the question, isn't it? How much is our brother's mind clouded by love for you—or by your magic. What better way to push him than to dangle his former mistress in front of him? And you."

She forced herself to eat, though Natly's tone wavered between pleading and strident, growing loud enough for certain words to be audible. Love. Wedding. Arill. Loyalty.

"Why are you helping me?" She asked Arnon. "I thought you didn't approve of me either."

"Is that what I'm doing?" Arnon's happy-go-lucky smile dropped, showing the canny expression beneath. "I think I'm just interested in your true colors, as well."

"I don't know what to do." She really hoped Chuffta had wise advice for this.

"Hair-burning is still an option."

"You are supposed to advise me! Make yourself useful."

"I submit that hair-burning would put an end to this very quick-ly. But," her Familiar added hastily when she mentally growled at him, *"it seems to me this is all theater, right? That's what Arnon is telling you. Lonen's brothers are playing old games, pulling on his tail to make him lose control. He'll look weak, unable to decide between his females. Not something a king should do."*

She agreed with that. *"I still don't know how I play in."*

"If you were what they think you to be—a spy, controller of their king, pursuing your own agenda to expose the Destrye so the Bárans can triumph—what would you do?"

"I'd encourage the chaos. If a scenario weakened Lonen, I'd work to increase that pressure."

"So, do the opposite."

Gah. More easily thought than accomplished. She needed time to think, which she didn't have, as the argument contin-ued to escalate. Natly stood now, nails flashing as she gesticulated. Nolan pounded his mug on the table, face screwed up as he scowled at Lonen, stabbing a finger at his chest. The people of the hall watched with avid delight, as if witnessing a mummer's play. Arnon sat back, sipping his wine, not watching the passionately involved trio, but observing her. Even Salaya seemed to have woken from her daze, her gaze alert and interested.

"They planned this—Arnon and Nolan."

"Oh yes, I think so."

Her temples throbbed, the relaxation of the aswae lost to the violent emotions churning around her with such potency they penetrated even her tightly closed shields, as if seeping into the pores of her skin like the warmed oils. She'd become permeable. Far from her home, far from the magic that had always sustained her. And for what?

These people respected nothing but strength. Much as the Bárans respected only power. They were the same thing, really—one physical, the other non-physical. Both with huge impacts.

She didn't have to pretend to be something she wasn't, to show herself to be truly on Lonen's side. She was as much the enemy of the King of Bára as any Destrye. Never mind that he was her brother.

That just made it more personal. The seething rage that burgeoned at the thought of Yar helped bolster her.

"Okay, fly about, breathe some flame—don't set anything on fire!—but make a spectacle. No hair-burning."

She caught barely the edge of Chuffta's glee as he surged off her shoulder with a clap of wings—and a keening howl unlike any other sound she'd ever heard him make. The cry morphed into a stream of fire that followed his path in a spiral, lingering in the air almost like smoke, to then sparkle gradually down on the ducking, and utterly shocked, Destrye.

Even Lonen fell silent, staring in astonishment.

Oria might have, too, had she not been concentrating on her own show. Keeping her focus on that sense of the silently breathing forest, she reached for the gift it had given her, and spun the living sgath—for sgath it was, just of another flavor, something to contemplate later—channeling it into active grien. Never having been trained in the supposedly exclusively male magic, she didn't have many prepared tricks up her sleeve, but she'd improvised before. Tossing her spoon into the air, she hit it midflight with a burst of grien, infusing the wood with growth energy long lost from its cells, but not forgotten. She stuck with the easiest path, letting it be what it had always been—so it sprouted tufts of new leaves, bright green with distant spring. Catching it neatly in her hand, she stepped past a wary Lonen and astounded Nolan, and offered the leafy twig to Natly, who gripped the arms of her chair, glossy red mouth in an O of horror or shock, or who knew.

"Natly," Oria said, "I owe you the gift of an apology. You've graciously given up the right to the promises King Lonen made you so that our people might be joined in peace. Please accept this token of my regard. It will remain ever green and bring you luck, prosperity, and fertility." She hoped so, anyway. If not, Oria would do her best to infuse the twig with new feedings of grien as often as possible.

Finally, tentatively, Natly lifted a hand and took it, at first touching it as she might a snake. Then a slow smile twitched at her mouth, spreading into something warm and genuine. "We grew these trees on my home farm."

Sheer luck there. Perhaps Lonen's goddess did smile on them. "Keep it in good health, for good memories."

The room remained hushed, so Oria picked up another wooden spoon, tossing it into the air and hitting it with another dollop of judicious grien. This one burst into blossom, small, pink and sweet, carrying the hint of crisp fruit to come. Oria took it to Salaya. "Princess Salaya. Nothing can replace the husband you lost, the father your sons will never know, but please accept this gift from me. May we come to know each other as sisters, and our joined families blossom as this does."

Salaya, dark eyes soft with welling tears, took the flowering twig, spinning it between her fingers. Oria left her with it.

And swiped Arnon's spoon on the way. She smiled at Lonen, who narrowed his eyes at her in some sort of warning, though admiration glinted in them, and tossed the spoon to the straw-covered floor behind the king's chair. Using the last of the magic she'd pulled in, she poured all of it into the dead wood, urging it to put down roots, to grow again.

At first nothing happened, except that the spoon seemed to worm its way through the straw, disappearing into the earth. Perhaps she'd miscalculated and the earth beneath the Destrye palace fortress remained too frozen for anything to grow.

But then, with a huge cracking sound, a sapling shot from the floor, fast as lighting and with the attendant rumbles. No, that was the awed murmuring of the gathering.

The sapling thickened, growing fatter, then taller, then fatter again by leaps, sprouting twigs like a fuzzy crown of baby's hair that rapidly became gracefully arching branches. The sound of the crowd grew, people leaping to their feet to point, and Lonen rose, taking her by the arm over her plush sleeve. The tightness of his grip communicated something, the excited leap of his emotions telling her more.

She would have slowed the astonishing growth, but couldn't. She'd given it everything she'd collected from that solemn chorus of breathing forest, and had nothing more to offer. Nor could she take it back. The limbs attenuated, draping from the central trunk nearly like vines.

Then, with a nearly audible chime, the umbrella of draping branches burst into a constellation of golden flowers, their sweet perfume bursting through the room.

The people gasped, then sent up a roar.

Lonen gripped her arm harder. "What have you done?"

~ 10 ~

A HALIGNE TREE. How had Oria known—or had she? She gazed up at him, copper eyes lustrous with the magic she'd wielded, though already the shadows deepened around them with its spending, face pale with trepidation at whatever she saw in his.

Up to him to explain this last gift then. She'd done it to stop the brewing fight—for which he was grateful, so far as observing protocols, even as he burned with frustrated ire to battle it out with them already. Nolan and Natly had baited him, yes, but he was Arill-cursed done with their poking him at every turn. *You don't need to think about if you're good enough to be king, because you* are *king.* Why couldn't Nolan just accept that reality?

And Natly. Of course she wouldn't give up without a struggle. The Destrye women might not be the sort of warriors who rode into battle, but they fought as fiercely as any man—and as tenaciously. He supposed he couldn't fault Natly for showing the same determination that won Bára for Dru, despite all odds.

But he'd see to it that she conceded defeat now. Oria had temporarily disarmed her. Salaya also, which made him wonder what encounter they'd had. Oria would be explaining a great deal. Once they extracted themselves from this fraught dinner. For all he knew, golems would spring from the earth next.

As soon as he thought it, he sent a swift prayer to Arill to guard against such an event. Knowing about the tunnels...if Oria could root a tree in the floor of the great hall, what would stop a burrowing golem from getting inside. They'd have no place of retreat then.

"And this tree, my queen?" he asked in a raised voice that commanded attention. "A gift to all the Destrye, Arill's own Haligne tree, carrying her sacred bloom. A promise of spring and bounty to come."

Her lashes lowered slightly in acknowledgement and perhaps relief. "Yes, Your Highness." She opened her mouth to say more, closing it again as Chuffta landed on her shoulder. Probably wise.

Nolan struggled to his feet, gripping the back of his chair and staring at the tree, looking both ill and awed. Arnon stroked his beard, arms otherwise folded, deep in thought.

"She can do this?" Nolan forced between his teeth, face darkening with anger. Here it came. "Your pet sorceress has the ability to grow fruit trees from nothing at all."

"Not nothing," Oria corrected, "I used—"

But Lonen, realizing he already held her arm in a fierce grip, released it and stopped her words by putting his arm around her shoulders. "One of Oria's magical gifts, yes, but—"

"All this time," Nolan grated out, his voice rising, "you've led us to believe that she'd wield battle magics to drive off mythical dragons, and you knew she could have been growing food right here in this very hall."

"Except for the minor issue of her being unconscious and weak from her journeys," Lonen shot back.

"She doesn't look weak now. And she's hardly been an

unconscious prize in your bed, fucking your brains out while you let your people starve."

"That's not exactly how—"

"Then how *is* it, little brother? Explain this to me because as I see it, I'm looking at a selfish man fatally distracted by a bit of foreign pussy when he should be serving his Arill-cursed people!" Nolan thrust a clenched fist at the stunned silent room. Arnon started forward, stopped himself.

Lonen, also, fought himself, wanting nothing more than to strike a blow across his brother's mouth that spoke so foully of Oria. Nolan and Ion, both, so certain that could be his only attraction to Oria. Unless his mind was controlled by her magic. Or whatever trumped-up reason they devised for what they simply didn't understand.

Couldn't understand because he still didn't dare expose Oria's weakness. How she'd summoned this much magic, he didn't know, but it had obviously tapped her out. Just in case, he asked, only for her ears, "Can you access more magic right now?"

She shook her head slightly, lips pressed together, tinged violet with fatigue.

"We're waiting for this answer, Lonen, and—"

"Your Highness," he corrected, overly loud but there it was. "I am your king, brother, whether you like it or not and you will address me and my wife with the appropriate respect."

"I do not like it!" Nolan roared. "This foul sorceress who toys with us and taunts us with Arill's sacred objects, profaning them with her Báran magic, she is no wife to you and you are no king of mine."

Silence, thick and jagged, fell hard across the room like a tree dropped by ice.

Very softly, Arnon groaned low in his throat. Oria held still as death against Lonen's side.

"Do you challenge me then, brother?" Lonen kept the words low enough to be between them, but the sound carried in the avidly listening hall.

"You have forced me to it," Nolan replied, stiff, head high, looking past Lonen to some vision only he could see. "I have no choice."

Now Arnon did move forward, taking Nolan by the arm. "You *do* have a choice," he hissed in his brother's ear. "Don't do this to us, to the Destrye, to Dru."

Nolan shook him off. "I'm doing this *for* the Destyre and Dru."

"The enemy is out there, man, not in here," Arnon urged in a harsh whisper.

"She is also here in this hall, along with any who aid her," Nolan replied, his gaze on Oria.

"The sorceress can help us; don't you see?"

"I see. Oh yes, I see all too clearly. And she *will* help us. Make no mistake of that. She will grow the crops we need to feed our people, but as penance for her people's crimes against us, not from the luxury of our king's bed. She clearly must be properly governed and controlled. Not coddled by a weak and besotted fool." He spat the last at Lonen.

"I would never be ruled by you," Oria hurled at him. "You make a grave mistake by thinking so." Lonen squeezed her, not to silence her this time, but in reassurance. He wouldn't let it happen, but her ferocity in the face of such a grim fate made him proud. His Báran sorceress was a warrior, too, in her own way.

"Do I, sorceress? We shall see. And the goddess will decide." Nolan's eyes glittered as he tightened his jaw. "I think you will do a great deal to protect your love from the death he's earned. It's clear from tonight's demonstration that you do care for him, regardless of your other plans. So, I challenge you, Lonen, son of Archimago and Vycayla according to the ancient laws. May Arill bestow her blessing on her chosen king."

"I accept your challenge, Nolan, son of Archimago and Vycayla according to the ancient laws," Lonen answered in tones loud enough to ring confidently through the hall, though the prospect made him ill inside. By the expression on Arnon's face, he felt the same.

Then Lonen's gut dropped, remembering his younger brother's warning, as Nolan clapped a hand over Arnon's where he gripped his arm. "Brother, will you stand second for me?"

Arnon looked away from Nolan, to Lonen, quiet anguish in his shadowed eyes. Of course his younger brother had no choice. He had to stand second for one or the other—and Lonen could forgive him the betrayal where Nolan never would. They both knew it.

"Yes," Arnon said quietly. "Yes, I will."

LONEN HUSTLED THEM down the hall, apparently back to their chambers, fast enough that Oria grew breathless keeping up, though she'd never complain. He gave orders as they went, summoning various people, by the names she caught. Uncharacteristically for him when she was present, he spoke in rapid-fire Destrye rather than in Common Tongue. Expediency or old habit, it didn't matter.

Events had turned as grim as they could be.

"Well, they could *be worse,"* Chuffta noted. *"The Trom could attack."*

"Shut up, Chuffta, really."

"It would be an excellent time, is all I'm saying. With the Destrye divided by internal strife, Yar would have the perfect opening. It's almost as if you did *do what they suspected."*

"Not. Helping."

He seemed to realize the depth of her displeasure belatedly. *"Of course we all know you didn't."*

Did they? By the grim set of Lonen's jaw, he might not see things that way. *"Just...don't talk to me right now."*

She'd messed it all up entirely. They entered his chambers and she turned to him, "Lonen, I—"

"Go sit by the fire," he interrupted. "Have some warmed wine or your cursed fruit juice. You're cold as ice and pale as death."

Okay, then. She did as he ordered, trying to be meek and unobtrusive—and also because sitting by the fire would feel good. The warm clothes had helped, but the great hall had been chilly, even before she unwisely spent the magic that left her empty. She sent Chuffta to his rug on the floor and tucked a fur blanket around herself. Some thoughtful soul had left spiced wine warming over a small candle, so she poured a mug and cupped the metal in her hands. It quickly became nearly hot enough to burn her palms, but she welcomed the sting. In the outer room, Lonen's voice rose and fell as he spoke with someone. Then the door closed and silence crept in from the corners.

Punishment for her crimes.

At last he came in, no longer wearing his formal clothes,

nor the wreath that named him king. He always took it off as soon as he could, it seemed, complaining of its weight. She'd picked it up once, when he was otherwise occupied, and it had felt light as a jewelbird in her hands. There could be all kinds of heaviness, though, she supposed.

Lonen sat heavily, bracing his forearms on his knees and lacing his fingers together, staring into the fire. He'd stripped down to a sleeveless shirt and breeches, his muscled arms and shoulders bare, along with his lower legs and feet. Old scars showed white against his tanned skin, the newer, still healing ones shades of pink and red, a map of his brutal history.

And now he'd fight for his life again, because of her.

Chuffta, curled in his blanket nest, but head up and alert, cocked his head, green eyes glowing bright with some thought he didn't send.

"Where did you get the magic?" Lonen asked finally.

She swallowed hard against the surprise. Not what she'd expected him to ask. "I… absorbed it earlier today. On the way to the aswae, we crossed a bridge and then in Arill's Temple I held a leaf and… it's difficult to explain."

He tilted a sideways look at her, gray eyes calm, expression so opaque she nearly opened a portal to read his thoughts. "Try," he suggested drily.

Fine. "I held this beautiful leaf—"

"That beautiful leaf?" He pointed to where the leaf she'd picked up sat on a lovely golden metal stand on the fireplace mantel.

"Yes." In all the flurry of preparation for dinner, she'd forgotten to look for it.

"It's a dead leaf, Oria."

"Remember five seconds ago when I told you it was hard to explain?" she bristled.

He chuckled, surprising her yet again, shaking his head. "Oh, good, you're still you. I was concerned someone had replaced my fiery sorceress wife with a milkmaid."

"I imagine milkmaids have challenges, too, what with cranky bulls."

"Milk comes from cows, not bulls," he corrected.

What did she know about livestock? "Cranky cows then."

"I'll allow as there are cows easily as mean as bulls out there." Now his eyes sparked with humor and she huffed at him.

"I don't know how you can jest at a time like this!"

He shrugged his shoulders, a slight roll, muscles flexing. "My father always said if you couldn't afford to despair, then your other choice was to laugh."

"Aha. This is where you get the eternal optimism from."

Lonen frowned slightly. "You know, I'd never have said so, but you could be right. He was the one who risked everything to take every able warrior to Bára on the word of a few scouts and with no hope of victory. It's amazing, really, that he convinced us all to go."

"Was there arguing—like tonight?"

"No. No one dared argue with my father. No one would have dared challenge him. He was a great warrior and king."

Her heart ached for the bleakness in his tone. "I'm so very sorry about tonight."

He glanced at her, raising his brows in surprise. "Why? It wasn't your fault."

It wasn't? "Sure it was—if I hadn't worked that magic…"

"It *would* have been helpful if you'd warned me."

"I didn't know myself! I only wanted to stop the brawl and it felt like I had enough magic—which, yes, I somehow absorbed from communing with the leaf and feeling this sense of—don't laugh—the forest breathing sgath into me."

He didn't laugh—instead he grinned. "Aha! Just as I'd hoped."

"What? Hoped how?"

"I told you before I thought you could absorb sgath from the trees. They're very old and powerful. And I kind of know what you mean. I've had that feeling when I've been in the forest—the usual sounds fall away and there's this deep vibration, like an enormous heart beating at a pace so even and slow that we aren't really aware of it most of the time."

She regarded him thoughtfully, taking a long sip of the warmed wine. "You're an odd man, Destrye," she finally said, and he tipped his head in acknowledgment.

"You wouldn't be the first to think so."

"And I thought you wanted me to absorb sgath from the lakes."

"We'll try them, too."

"We—when? What are you talking about?"

He finally sat back, scrubbing his hands on his thighs. "We leave in the morning."

"We—I—you—" She was sputtering.

"Yes," he nodded helpfully. "You and me makes we, and Chuffta, too. And Buttercup. The old team together again." He sounded wry about that.

"But the challenge—are you forfeiting or... running away?"

His gaze went flinty. "Have you ever known me to run away from any challenge, Sorceress—including the formidable ones you set me?"

"No." Unaccountably a laugh welled up in her chest, but she held it down, savoring the bright sense of well-being it brought. It did her heart good to see him back to his arrogant self, though she couldn't account for the change in him. "Then what—"

"The sgath you got from that dead leaf, is it enough?"

"It wasn't just the leaf."

"Is it enough, Oria?"

"It depends. Enough for what?" But she knew.

"How about growing food in the hall—can you do that?"

"Well, not yet, but—"

"So we're going to find a better source."

"*But*, I was going to say, I'm working on it. I just need time to refine the technique, to meditate on it."

Lonen was shaking his head, his expression full of regret. "We're out of time, unfortunately. Not just for growing food. I need you to—"

"Your Highness?" An older man's voice called from the outer chamber and Lonen sprang to his feet.

"In here, Priest Robson," Lonen called out, waving to Oria to remain seated.

An older Destrye entered the room. Not a warrior, but tall as any of them, his wild mane of hair gone purest white with age. His brows, too, bristled with long white hairs that curled with untamed glee, as did his drooping beard and mustache. He wore deep green robes like Talya's and fixed interested pale blue eyes on her.

"Rhiten, may I present my wife, Oria, Sorceress of Bára," Lonen said in the most respectful tone she'd ever heard him use.

"Not your wife, boy. Not until Arill seals the union with her gentling hand." Despite his attenuated appearance, Priest Robson had a voice full of vigor. He never took his eyes off Oria.

"I made the vow," Lonen said, and the priest raised his

brows, making the strands rearrange themselves into starbursts. "Arill's vow, warrior to wife."

"I know which vow you meant, boy," the priest replied irritably. "You had no business doing that without a priest or priestess there to witness."

"I didn't have one handy," Lonen replied in that dry tone of his. "And we'd already married under Báran law and magic, so it seemed … redundant."

Which vow was this? Oria cast back her mind. When she'd hesitated to confide the secrets that would get her killed, he'd knelt, kissed the hem of her robes and made a promise. *I swear by the magic that binds us, by the seed of me in you and the blossom of you in me, that I shall never betray you, my wife, whether by action or inaction.*

"'Redundant,' he says." The priest snorted and cast his eyes skyward. "Arill save us from impetuous boys who think they can decide which rituals to keep and which to discard. Báran, are you, girl?"

"Yes, Priest Robson," she ventured, though that answer seemed obvious enough. She felt wrong, sitting curled up under her blanket, but Lonen had told her to stay put, so she stayed.

"Hmm. Saw your display in the great hall. Quite the show."

She didn't know what to say to that, so she held her tongue and he transferred that pale gaze to Chuffta. "And this creature—it does your bidding? I've heard tell of witches who keep animal assistants to work magic for them, serve as repositories of power, that sort of thing."

A tingle ran down her spine. "I am no witch; I'm a sorceress."

He made a noise that might have been simply clearing a

stopped nostril, though she doubted it. "What's the difference?"

"There's no such thing as witches," she replied evenly, "except perhaps in children's tales."

Priest Robson scowled and harrumphed, but let the topic drop there. He turned back to Lonen, opened a book he carried and began reading in the Destrye dialect.

Oria took advantage of the opportunity to confer with Chuffta. *"Have you heard of Familiars acting as repositories of magic before?"*

"Oh, am I allowed to speak to you again?" Chuffta's mind-voice reeked of disdain.

"Don't be a suck-sand. I needed a moment of peace is all."

"I'm sorry I said the wrong thing."

"Don't be. I was wrong to tell you to shut up."

"Then I have heard some derkesthai tales along those lines, but they always sounded like legends. Like the stories of derkesthai drinking from magic springs and growing to ten times their normal size."

Her skin went clammy. *"You mean… the size of Trom dragons?"*

Chuffta went very quiet. Finally, *"I never thought of it that way."*

"I thought you told me you're not related to those monsters."

"We're not!" He sounded fully insulted.

"You said it was like comparing a house cat to one of the golden desert jaguars."

"Exactly."

"But those are related creatures—just different in size and wildness."

"And intelligence. Don't forget that the Trom dragons are stupid beasts that lack derkesthai intelligence."

"How do you know?"

"Why else let the Trom ride them?"

"That's no answer."

He stayed silent a moment, then, sulkily, *"They* look *stupid."*

She was saved coming up with a reasonable reply to that by Lonen and Priest Robson turning to her.

"If you think she's up to it, boy, and you think you can get Her Eminence to assist, then I'll play my part."

"She's up to it," Lonen assured him.

Those spectacular brows drew together, sending them into an even more impressive pattern. "What say you, sorceress—you're willing?"

Oria looked past him to Lonen, who nodded encouragement. *Trust me.* Oh well, not like she had any other options at this point. "I'm willing."

"All right then. Travel safely under Arill's hand." The priest closed the text with a thump, nodded decisively, and left without another word.

Oria waited for the sound of the outer door closing. "What did I just agree to?"

Lonen came to her, standing behind her chair and filling his hands with her hair, sliding his fingers through it. She'd become so accustomed to this lulling ritual that her eyes half-closed, and she wanted to purr like one of Chuffta's house cats. "It means more than I can express," Lonen said, in soft, slightly rough voice, "that you agreed without knowing."

She shrugged a little, tipping her head back to look up at him through her lashes. Her fierce warrior. They were in it together, for better or worse. "You asked me to trust you."

"I appreciate the leap. I know that's not easy for you."

Perhaps not—but easier every moment she spent with

him, it seemed. "So what did I agree to?"

"You're going to be my second in the duel."

Her eyes flew open wide. "I'm what? I can't do that!"

"There's no one else I'd rather have at my back. Priest Robson checked ancient law, and in the absence of other immediate family able and willing to serve as my second, my wife can fill the role."

"I'm no warrior—I can't fight your brothers."

"With magic you can."

"But…" She trailed off, realizing. *Travel safely under Arill's hand.* "That's why you asked if there was enough magic in the leaf. And why we're journeying to find a better source—or for me to confront the wild magic."

"Yes. Also, we need a sponsor for our wedding in Arill's Temple, since Nolan has lodged a protest to the marriage, along with tonight's challenge. We need someone with greater authority than he has."

"Don't you, as king?"

"I did, but no longer—not with the challenge live. Until we resolve it, we're equal in authority."

"That sounds like an unreasonable system."

"It's an old system," he admitted. "But typically a challenge would not be left unresolved for long. It would either be settled immediately or at first light the following day."

That's why he'd hustled them out of the great hall so fast. "So Nolan expects you to fight in the morning?"

"Yes, be we won't be here. Baeltya will be here soon to give us one more treatment that will last a while, then we'll sneak out before dawn."

"Won't that be you conceding the challenge?"

"No. Priest Robson confirmed that Nolan must wait seven days to declare me dead."

"He was thought dead longer than that," she pointed out.

Lonen rubbed the scar around his eye. "So many men lost in the war, we never got around to the formality of declaring all the missing as dead. It seemed unnecessary at the time."

"And now we have to sneak out of your own palace."

His eyes sparkled. "It'll be fun. Like escaping Bára again."

"That was *not* fun."

"You felt very nice bouncing on my shoulder, your breasts all soft on my back, your adorable bottom high in the air."

She closed her eyes and groaned. "Only you."

"You love me for it."

"Maybe," she conceded. "So who has this higher authority to sponsor a wedding in Arill's Temple?"

"Someone fortuitously living very near the lake I planned to take you to."

A note of hesitation in his voice alerted her and she squinted at him. "*Who*, Lonen?"

He gave her a lopsided smile. "My mother. Her Eminence, the former Queen of the Destrye."

All she needed. One more impossible Destrye woman to make her life miserable.

~ 11 ~

A S PROMISED, LONEN woke her in the early hours, when all was dark and still.

Though how *he* knew the time, she couldn't fathom. Even had the windows been uncovered, there wouldn't be any hint of sunrise yet. Pilaryh came to help her dress and pack her final things—something that surprised her, until Lonen curtly told her he wouldn't give anyone access to her who wasn't utterly loyal.

Apparently, although he'd told Oria numerous times not to be concerned about Nolan's challenge, Lonen had been expecting it. She'd been through the same with Yar. Hoping one's potentially traitorous sibling wouldn't do the worst was one thing. Being blind to the possibility was another.

Pilaryh dressed her warmly in layers, including wonderful wool stockings lined with fur that went all the way up to her crotch, held up by ribbons attached around her waist. Short bloomers would allow her to answer the call of nature without having to get chilled. Knee-high boots, also fur-lined, would keep her feet warm. Then layers of skirts and wool petticoats, the light indoor cloak she'd worn to dinner, and then another that Lonen produced, made entirely of incredibly soft white fur.

She stroked it, wondering at the texture. It wasn't alabaster white, but had a dappled pattern when she turned it just so in the light. A kind of faint striping of shorter beige and gray hairs mixed in with the longer ones.

"What kind of animal did this come from?" She wondered aloud.

"You're not telling me you're going to refuse to wear it," Lonen said.

"Did I ask after its name? I'm wearing half a dozen creatures' former skins already," she retorted. "I'm hardly going to draw the line now. I was simply curious."

He ran his hand down the fall of her hair. "I apologize, love—I'm on edge. It's a shadowcat. They live in forests farther north. The color and dappling makes it ideal for blending with the snow. There's a hood as well, to cover your hair."

"There's your one for the day." She smiled at him. "I'll hardly be invisible when I'm otherwise wearing scarlet clothing, riding a big black warhorse, and hanging out with a fearsome Destrye warrior."

Lonen grinned. "There are times to stay hidden and others to been seen in powerful ways. We'll be doing both."

THEY CREPT OUT of the palace, Chuffta scouting ahead of Alby—though the guards on duty who saw them looked steadily past. Lonen and his loyal attendants. How did he assess who would keep his secrets? She wouldn't have known in Bára. Well, at least she hadn't until the city fell to the Destrye and she found herself having to make decisions. At that point, most people had made clear where they stood. Some offered unequivocal loyalty, others—like her perfidious brother—made everything more difficult for her.

The tricky ones were those who seemed to change like a flower that follows the sun, forever adjusting to face whoever held the most power.

Banked fires lit a few rooms, but only enough to make the enormous log walls loom like sleeping giants. A few guards manned the great doors, opening them just enough when Alby spoke to them for their stealthy party to slip through, the snick of the locks behind them loud in her ears. She hadn't much liked being closed in, unablt to look out of the windows, but by the time they exited the final door, Oria felt exposed, and not only because the chill settled against her skin.

Below, the shanty town gleamed here and there with lanterns. Mostly, though, the pre-dawn dark loomed with oppressive, cold quiet. To the side, Buttercup whuffed a greeting, steaming breath billowing out, and she skipped with glee to see him, cupping his big head in her gloved hands and blowing softly into his nostrils. The groom who'd brought him made a sound of distress, throwing out a hand to stop her, but Lonen told the boy not to be concerned.

Slipping off one glove to feel the warhorse's mind better, Oria leaned against him. Buttercup would never harm her. He smelled of sweet hay and heat, his mind fierce, eager—and excited for what the day might bring, much like Lonen's state of mind. Buttercup didn't think in focused words as Chuffta did, but he possessed a certain kind of sense. He seemed pleased to see the derkesthai, too, huffing and bobbing his head when Chuffta landed on the saddle and snaked his head around to peck at the horse's neck in affection.

"Up you go," Lonen whispered to her, grasping her by the

waist and lifting her into the saddle, Chuffta winging up to clear the way. The groom held Buttercup still for them, so she didn't need to. Even with Lonen's height and strength, she had to grab hold of the saddle and haul herself onto the massive stallion. "Scoot forward," Lonen murmured, then was up behind her before she knew it.

"I'm riding in front?" she asked. "The saddle feels different."

"I had it redesigned." His breath caressed her ear as he leaned to speak into it, a warm shiver going through her. He rearranged her shadowcat cloak, more forward, snugging her up in the vee of his powerful thighs and adjusting his own cloak around them both. Wrapping an arm around her waist for good measure, he took the reins and nodded to Alby.

"If anyone asks," he said quietly, "you know only that your king requested his steed and left, nothing more."

"All know I do your bidding, Your Highness. There's no crime in that loyalty," Alby replied with hushed fervency. "May Arill hold you in her palm and grant your swift return to take and hold the throne, my king."

"Good man." Maybe Lonen's voice roughened a bit because of the need for quiet, but Oria suspected there was more to it.

They rode through the maze of buildings, hoods up, Buttercup stepping with that stealth so uncanny for his size and boisterous nature. They crossed a bridge over the moat. As Pilaryh had told her—it was filled not with water but with sharp spears all pointing toward the perimeter. The road crossed a short cleared area, then passed between two huge trees that stood as quiet and unmoving as the sentries back at the palace. As the lantern light disappeared behind them, the shadows of the deep, old forest settled around them, only the faint gleam of snow and Chuffta's ghostly form showing against all the shades of black.

Somewhere beyond that dense canopy of limbs, the moons would be in the sky. At least Grienon, in his swift passage. Sgatha might have lumbered already beyond the rim of the world, not to return for some time. Oria had lost track of the moon cycles, even time itself.

"More room," Lonen said, as if they'd only paused in the conversation, "to put the saddle bags and supplies behind me, and better for Buttercup to have the weight back over his haunches. Also," he squeezed her waist, "I feel better having you where I can hold on to you."

"I'm not going to fall off—my seat is much better than that by now. I could probably have ridden my own horse."

"This is faster and safer." He dropped a hand against her bottom and squeezed again, nuzzling against her hood. "And more fun. Though I'll agree your seat is excellent."

"Is sex all you think about?" she tried to sound tart, but his flirting warmed her. It was nice to be just them again, without all the people around.

"Not all," he sounded close. "When you're not anywhere I can see you or touch you or smell you, then I think about other things."

"Like redesigning saddles and which of your people are loyal enough to compile supplies and sneak us out of the palace."

"Those things, too," he agreed. "I also think up ways for us to pleasure each other, now that we're both healthier."

"Unfortunately, all your scheming has resulted in us no longer having a bed."

"I think something can be arranged."

"In the middle of a forest?"

"You'll see."

"Tell me." But he refused to say more about it.

She dozed a bit, then woke to growing light, perfectly warm between Lonen and Buttercup's combined body heat, along with the lusciously soft fur of her cloak. If only she could wear it all the time, she'd never get cold. Perhaps she could have more garments made of the shadowcat fur? She had to mentally shake her head at herself—what a long way she'd come from refusing to eat meat on principle to contemplating how to divest more shadowcats of their hides.

"We all live at the expense of something else," Chuffta pointed out from wherever he flew above or beyond them. *"It's neither good nor bad. It just is."*

"I just feel like I'm becoming more Destrye all the time—barbarian and predatory."

"Bára preyed on the Destrye, who definitely have names."

He had an excellent point. Perhaps she'd always been the worse predator, like the great cats, hunters so lethal they could afford to spend most of their time napping in the sun. An image uncomfortably close to how her life in Bára had been, lolling in the shade of silk screens during the heat of the afternoon, the lush luxury of her garden, the beauty of the city.

"You're forgetting all the time you spent studying, meditating, training to be a priestess and striving for hwil *in order to master your magic."*

She had sort of forgotten some of that, how intensely critical mastering her magic had seemed back then, how attaining her mask had seemed more important than anything in the world. As small as her world had been then, she supposed the mask had loomed that large. Since then she'd gained the mask and lost it just as quickly—and so many concerns loomed far larger.

Perhaps that's how life worked. She'd left the worries of her girlish self behind, maybe washed away by the bore tides of Bára, and she had the concerns of a woman now. One day she might have the thoughts of a queen, or a mother, or a crone. Strange to consider.

For now, it was good to be in the moment.

The light grew brighter, not just from the sun rising. The forest had thinned, with the trees slighter here, more spaced out. The road they followed approached a clearing. Though snow covered it all, the burnt remnants of what must have been a good-sized house tumbled black and collapsed. An extensive garden had been laid out, with barns beyond and still-standing fences that ringed empty paddocks containing only pristine snow. Nothing stirred.

It all reminded her forcibly of the images in Baeltya's mind, of the people and animals bleeding and crying all around the little farm. Not this one, but very like it.

"What happened here?" she asked, though she knew.

"Golems," Lonen confirmed. "Years ago, though. Before we set out to find Bára. And not necessarily an actual golem incursion. Most of these outlying farms were abandoned as water supplies dried up and because it was simply too risky to be so far away from help."

"Do you know that's what happened here for sure?"

"No, I don't know which family had this place. I never had much occasion to pay attention to such things." He had a frown in his voice for that.

"Then how are you so certain?" The road curved around the desolate farm, climbing a hill behind it.

"Mostly logic. We've been riding at a good pace for about three hours—and Buttercup's walk is faster than most horses. That means a rider going for help at a flat out run would take that amount of time to get to the palace and back, which is much too long. Also, the gates are closed on the paddocks, which means an orderly evacuation."

"But they burned the house?" She studied it again. Knowing how careful the Destrye were with flame, it seemed unlikely to be an accident.

"Ah." Lonen was silent a moment. This time when he snugged up against her, it felt more like him seeking comfort than flirtation. "That no doubt happened when the Trom attacked."

Oh. "They attacked here—this little farm?"

"Yes and no. Wait a moment, and you'll see."

They continued along the road, which ascended more steeply. The deep woods returned, the huge trunks full of their own quiet. But among them now were scattered boulders and the occasional jagged upthrust of rock. Granite, the color of Lonen's eyes. Buttercup's breath billowed in clouds by the time they reached the summit of the switchbacking trail, and the trees abruptly gave way to a startling vista.

The stood at the edge of a dramatic drop, the land below a flat stretch of snow-covered fields, patchworked by an array of wooden fences. Some sections of them had collapsed, others had burned and ended in nothing but snow. If she could reach out a hand to brush the snow away, there would be scars of burn and ash continuing in a line along the ground.

Lonen dismounted and held his arms up to lift her down, steadying her when her cramped legs protested, stiff after a few hours of riding. "I've already lost my riding endurance," she muttered.

"You'll get it back quick enough. The first day is always the hardest. And Buttercup might have a pansy name, but he's a big horse." Lonen slapped the warhorse on the shoulder with affection, sending him to lip at the snow in the pockets of grass along the otherwise windswept cliff's edge.

"It's not a pansy name—a buttercup is another flower entirely—and I don't see what his being a big horse has to do with it."

Lonen leered at her, patting her bottom. "Every woman walks funny after having a big stallion between her legs."

She swatted at him. "Get you out of the palace and you turn into a randy boy, all hands and dirty jokes."

He grimaced cheerfully at that. "You might have a point there, love. I feel like a new man, getting out of that place. The weight of all those decisions, everyone watching me all the time, wanting things from me, evaluating everything I say and do." He subsided, rubbing at the scar by his eye, then shrugged it off. "Anyway, come look."

"I can't help seeing," she said, but she walked to the edge with him and let him draw her against his side. Beyond the extensive meadows below, the forest resumed again, hills rolling in the distance, the trees blurring into a frost of brown merging with the gray sky. Chuffta glided on a thermal rising along the drop, humming his happiness at the lovely glide. "Is all of this Dru?"

"More or less as far as the eye can see," he agreed. "Though we don't draw boundaries as such. Once upon a time the Destrye had no settlements. Our ancestors traveled constantly, carrying their few possessions on their backs, following the game animals through the seasons."

"Raiding cities and carrying off foreign women," she inserted in a dry tone.

He hugged her and kissed the fur next to her temple. "If they got very, very lucky."

She had to laugh, but sobered. "So you traveled all this

land, but eventually settled here."

"And near the other forts. These fields were Arill's first, cleared by the goddess's own hand to feed her children so that we might settle down and follow gentler ways."

She cocked her head up at him. He had his hood pushed back, so the frost accumulated on his dark curling hair, the haft of his battle-axe protruding over one shoulder, ever at hand. In this light, his face looked harsh, the scars standing stark in deep lines, as he gazed over the land as one of his fierce ancestors might have. "Enough with the nonsense, Destrye," she teased. "Surely you don't believe a goddess actually removed the trees so your ancestors could farm."

He glanced down, eyes soft gray with sober affection. "Why not? My powerful sorceress wife could do it."

That gave her pause. Lonen watched her with amusement while she struggled for a response. "There are differences between goddesses and sorceresses," she finally said.

"Such as?"

She punched his side, like hitting a wall with her gloved knuckles. "Divinity. Immortality. Unlimited power."

"There was a time we believed all of those things about the priests and priestesses of Bára."

And the Báran priests and priestesses liked to propagate that reputation, too.

"Think on this," he continued when she only hmm'd in thought. "Who's to say where the original concept of Arill came from? You ask me if I really believe that the goddess removed the trees with her own hands, and I don't know that I do. But I believe in Arill's teachings, that they mean something and come from somewhere. Or someone. Maybe some brute of a warrior Destrye carried off the wrong sorceress, fell in desperately in love with her—and who could blame him?—and she agreed to stay with him if he mended his more off-putting ways and didn't make her chase after deer all her life. Seems clearing a few trees would have been well worth the effort on her part."

"More than a few," Oria pointed out, but found herself measuring the distances, estimating what kind of magical resources it would take. Over time, it might be possible, even for one woman.

"They wouldn't have needed to do it all at once," Lonen said, echoing her thoughts. "They might have added a field at a time. By all accounts, the Destrye were not so many then."

Of course, they weren't so many now, but neither of them spoke those words aloud. "You've been thinking about this," she said instead. "This theory about Arill and sorceresses."

"Yes," he admitted. "I'm interested to find out if my memory is accurate—and to find out what you think when you see it."

"In the fields?"

"Oh no—we're not going that way. We could have reached the fields far more quickly by the low road. No, we're going that way." He turned her and pointed to where the hills rose higher and more jagged, ending in peaks, sharp against the sky. Fog swirled around them, then parted, a sun she couldn't see hitting the blinding white snow fields atop them.

She caught her breath, the bite cold in her lungs. "All the way up there?" she squeaked, making Lonen laugh.

"It's not so far as it appears."

"Is it as cold as it appears?"

"Yes, but not much colder than here. We'll stop for the night along the way and I'll keep you warm."

At least she wouldn't have to meet his mother on that very day. A small reprieve, but she'd take it. She returned her gaze to the fields. "Then down there is where the Trom attacked. That house burning was incidental. They did it on their way over the ridge—along with the crops and the aqueducts." Not fences then, but elevated wooden ditches to carry water to the fields. Refocusing her attention, she made out the paths of flame, where the edges of the forest had trees starkly black from fire, rather than winter. The pattern without the snow would be easier to see, but now that she aligned the view with what she'd glimpsed in Lonen's memories, the scene made more sense.

In her mind's eye, a stark black shape swooped over the fields, now golden with ripe grain. So easily fired, they leapt into gouts of flame, dark smoke billowing. The dragon sliced through it all, serene, graceful, and lethal. The figure on its back, a dark spider form, seemed to turn and look at her, matte eyes seeing deep into her mind.

We come when summoned. Don't forget.

She shook the vision away with an effort. They come when summoned. "What was their goal?"

"They burned our late harvest, and the aqueducts that brought water from the higher lakes." With his pointing finger, he traced for her where the aqueduct had ascended stepwise up a hill not far away. "The attack left us without that last crop and squelched any possibility of irrigating for a winter crop, even had the winter been not so cold. In the spring we'll have to do that much more work to rebuild the aqueducts. And that's if they don't come back to do it again. Which I think we both know they will."

She let him talk, though she knew all of that, had seen it. A memory drawn from what she'd glimpsed in Lonen's mind, one reconstructed from stories, or presentiment of the future? She didn't know. Some of all of that, perhaps. She let him lift her onto Buttercup's back. "But I still don't see what they hoped to achieve."

"Isn't that enough?" Lonen asked in that wry tone, vaulting up behind her. "Would you have had them burn the palace and Arill's Temple, too?"

"That would have made sense," she retorted. "If they wanted to destroy you utterly, that would have been a relatively simple step to doing so. Burn all the aqueducts—they made an easy visual line to follow. Instead, they did this patchwork attack—burn some aqueducts and not others. Burn that house but not the rest of the farm."

"What are you thinking their reasoning was?"

"I don't know. I don't understand the Trom, or the nature of the beasts they ride. They seem to do things for their own reasons."

"I thought they followed Yar's commands." Lonen urged Buttercup back up the road, and Chuffta shot overhead, an alabaster arrow. He said the flying kept him warmer than riding, but he'd be tiring soon enough and wanting to nap inside her furry cloak.

"Ostensibly they're supposed to," she mused, considering. "Though I don't know the mechanics of the summoning spell. The summoner—or summoners, as I think it takes both a male and female—command the loyalty of the Trom who respond, but I'm not sure how absolute that authority is. But even if we agree that Yar asked the Trom to come here to burn the fields and aqueducts, what purpose did that serve?"

"They did take water away."

"Which is a high priority for him. It means both life for Bára and power for him. But he could have had them collect the water without burning the crops. It would have been smarter not to burn the aqueducts and let you all do the work to make the water easily accessible."

"You're welcome." He sounded grim, so she patted his thigh pressed against hers, his muscle tightening in response.

"Not to be crass, but I'm trying to view it as he would."

"Understood. But it could be that the Trom simply like to burn things. When they arrived in Bára to save the city and drive us out, they killed Bárans and Destrye alike with their dragon fire."

"That's true." She shuddered at the horrible memory. "The Trom don't explain themselves. I was only told that they exact the price they wish to in exchange for their aid."

"So maybe they did it as a side bonus to grabbing some water for Yar. Burning us out here was fun for them." Lonen sounded neutral, but his old anger brooded dark beneath.

"Fire is fun," Chuffta commented. *"It's hot and bright."*

Oria didn't relay the troubling comment to Lonen, hiding even from her Familiar how much it unsettled her to contemplate his similarities to the giant and deadly Trom dragons.

~ **12** ~

THEY ARRIVED AT the chapel by midafternoon—sooner than his memories had predicted. It was only the pair of them, though, on a single horse. When he'd traveled this way in the past, it had always been with a mixed group, on steeds nowhere close to Buttercup's caliber. Their excursions back then had always been for pleasure, too, with much stopping along the way to picnic, climb trees, and take in the views.

Back before the golems came.

The chapel seemed smaller than in his memory, too, as if it had also shrunk along with the distance. Unlike most Destrye dwellings, this had been built of stone, the uneven rocks collected or hewn from the mountainside and painstakingly fitted together. Now that he saw it again, what he'd remembered as a fanciful design reminded him of Bára. Not in a way he could pin to specific details, but in the feel of it. As if it had been created to please someone with that aesthetic. Perhaps that boded well for the rest of what he thought he remembered about the place.

He dismounted, and Oria pushed back her hood, surveying the small chapel. The sun had finally broken through the overcast, and the rays hit her hair, radiating off the shining copper like a fire of the most benevolent kind. Her eyes, nearly as bright, held doubt, however, at the sight of the unprepossessing buildings. No indication she found it familiar. "We're stopping here?"

"For the night, yes."

Chuffta poked his narrow white head through the parting of her cloak, only the vivid green of his gaze a break in the alabaster on ivory shades. Oria smiled slightly, her expression changing as she conversed mentally with the dragonlet. Then she focused on Lonen again, the smile warming. "Chuffta says he sees a chimney in the cabin at the back and wonders if we'll need firewood." She arched her coppery brows in rueful amusement.

"There might be some stockpiled," he said to Chuffta. "But I'm guessing it's been a while since anyone has visited the place. We may need to chop more. How are you at chasing rodents, Chuffta man?"

Chuffta emerged fully, cocking his head with interest and shaking out his wings, nearly clipping Oria in the face with one. She was already choking on her reaction. "Rodents?" She squeaked out.

"They tend to nest in warm places like this," he told her in apology as he lifted her down.

"It doesn't look warm."

"Relatively speaking. We'll get a fire going and roust them out."

She nodded absently, face rapt as she turned in a slow circle. She felt it. He'd been certain she would. Okay, he hadn't been *certain*. Hopeful. "This is a good place," she murmured, almost to herself.

"Full of coherent sgath?"

Her face smoothed into that neutral mask. Her priestess face. Then her eyes fired again, full of keen intensity. "Not exactly. But something." She tipped her head back, following the spear of the straight, dark trunks to the blue sky, then closed her eyes, turning again and holding out her arms as she did. The parting of her white cloak over the scarlet gown beneath was like the sun breaking through the clouds all over again. She paused, facing away from the chapel to where the ground fell away to the gorge below, the peaks and lowering sun beyond.

Like Arill herself, some reverent part of him whispered.

Her eyes snapped open, startling him, they burned so incandescently in her winter-white face. "Is it safe here?" she asked.

"In what way?" he hedged, uncertain where she was going with this.

"I'd like to go deeper into the woods. By myself. To meditate." The smile she gave him at that was both self-conscious and teasing for his own dislike of the practice.

"I'll go with you."

But she shook her head. "I need to be alone. If that's okay with you," she added, with a touch of hesitation.

"Of course it's okay with me." He ran a hand over her shining hair, savoring the satin feel of it. It would give him time to set things up. "Take Chuffta with you."

"You need him for firewood. And rodent chasing," she added archly.

"I know how to chase out rodents."

"Yes, but you have him all interested now. I'll take him with me so he can see where I settle, then he can check back on me. I have a couple of hours of light left, yes?" She glanced uncertainly at the sun, which hovered over the far peaks.

He pointed for her. "It will set there, so yes, a couple of hours. Will it take that long?"

Her eyes sparkled and her face held a vivid anticipation he

hadn't seen in her for quite some time. "It might." She nodded, as if confirming to herself. "Very likely. But Chuffta can rouse me if you need me."

"Sounds good." Wishing he could kiss her, he cupped her head and hugged her to him. "You won't get cold?"

She stepped back and pulled up her hood, tucking back the fire of her hair until none of it showed, tugging the alabaster fringes so they hung long around her face. "In my lovely cloak? Never."

Answering her soundless summons, Chuffta bolted from above, folding his wings to land neatly on her shoulder, talons digging into the pad he'd had them sew into it. She walked away, the dappled cloak dragging over the snow, blurring her footprints, the derkesthai a slightly more iridescent shape in the panorama of white, punctuated only by the sacred black sentinels of the trees.

The scene struck him as spooky and magical at once, sending that numinous shiver through him that he'd first felt upon spying her in a window in Bára.

"Oria?" he called after her, and she turned, adding fire to the frozen landscape again with her copper eyes. "I'll be here waiting."

Her lips curved in a gentle smile. "I love you, too, Destrye."

As HE'D SUSPECTED, what little wood had been stockpiled had been scattered by wildlife during years of neglect. He found some dry pieces to start a fire with, however, buried under the snow in the lee of the cabin. Carrying it inside, he found the interior dusty, but thankfully unmolested.

Arill's followers built her waystations with care.

He laid fires in both the chapel and cabin, but waited on Chuffta to start them, as the little firebug enjoyed that so. Taking advantage in the interim, he opened all the doors to the cabin and attached chapel, removing the hides from the windows to shake them out, and allowing the cold mountain air to sweep through and clear out the stale.

He was tacking up the hides again—in spring, once the crops were planted, he'd have to send someone up here to replace them with newer, more supple ones, as these had grown brittle with cold and age—when Chuffta returned. Not for the first time, he wished he could talk to the derkesthai as Oria could, and ask after her. But what would he ask? Obviously she was fine, or her Familiar wouldn't be acting so relaxed. "She's a big girl," he muttered to himself. "And she survived just fine before you came along, buddy."

Chuffta flew up to him, hovering, and gave him a long look, then bobbed his head in that way that always made Lonen think he was winking at him. "Fires are laid, Chuffta man, if you'd like to do the honors."

With an enthusiastic spurt of green flame, the derkesthai shot over to the cabin fireplace, using quite a bit more than necessary to send the logs into an instant blaze. Lonen braced, half expecting the flames to escape the stones and attack the wood of the walls, but it settled back quick enough. Chuffta looked over his shoulder, as if to chide him for his lack of faith.

"In the chapel, too," he said, pointing through the doorway. At least that was all stone, so the fire-breathing dragonlet could go unsupervised. While Chuffta took care of that, Lonen found bedding in the chests made of insect-resistant wood, which had kept everything at least unchewed, and aired those out too.

Then he and Chuffta went to gather more wood. He'd brought a smaller axe, so he didn't have to shame his armsmaster's memory by using his weapon. He'd already rubbed down Buttercup and installed him in the attached stable, where the warhorse happily munched some oats he'd also brought along.

Journeying with supplies made everything worlds better.

He kept half an eye on the sun, feeling a bit like a fretful old nanny, but also cautious of becoming complacent. There was safe and there was *safe*. More predators than golems and Trom haunted these hills, especially in the crepuscular hours.

He made himself wait until the sun just touched the peak it would set behind, and was opening his mouth to ask Chuffta to check on Oria, when the purpling shadows between the trees shifted. Pale violet blurred into white—and she emerged.

She had her head bowed, in contemplation still or watching her footing, so he couldn't see her face past the furry fringe. Following impulse, he went to her and picked her up, holding her tight against him, his face pressed to her hood. She laughed, a bell-like melody he recalled from her garden in Bára, one he hadn't heard since. Magic ran through it, as if her happiness and pleasure grew out of her store of sgath, which perhaps it did.

Oria leaned back in his arms, arching to place her gloved hands on his cheeks, so she could search his face. "What's that for?"

"I missed you," he said simply, expecting a teasing reply, but she sobered, her laughing smile softening to a tender one.

"I missed you, too." The smile quirked to one side. "It occurs to me that we've not been much out of each other's company in the last days."

True. And the small separation had left him a little hollow. Not how he'd ever expected to feel about a woman. Well, about anyone. Needing to reconnect with her, he searched for what to say. What did one ask of a sorceress who went seeking meditation? It felt like she'd been hunting and he should inquire if she'd gotten the trophy bull she sought, though that metaphor was all wrong. Also, he didn't know much about magic, but it seemed like something that eluded her the more she forced it. The last thing she needed was more pressure.

"Did you find what you sought?" He finally asked.

She looked thoughtful, pushing at his shoulders, so he set her down. "Can we go inside? I *am* cold now."

"Of course." Surprising her, he picked her up again, but this time in the cradle of his arms, in the traditional style. Striding to the cabin, he kicked the door open, carried her over the threshold and set her on her feet inside.

"Now what was *that* for?" But she laughed as she said it, then he was saved answering as she took in the room with wide eyes. It had warmed up nicely, Chuffta vigilantly tending a fire that burned to the limit of the stone frame, thrilled to be given free rein. The freshened bed linens were turned back invitingly, furs piled at the end. The candles around the room in their shuttered lanterns scattered light with a warm glow and the table set for two boasted a small vase of bledsiae he'd found. She went to that, touching the hardy white blossoms. "Flowers?"

"They grow under the snow, at the base of the trees." He put his hands on her shoulders, looking at the flowers, too. "They reminded me of you."

She glanced up with narrowed eyes. "Small and frozen?"

"Hardy." He squeezed her shoulders, the bones light as a kitten's under the shadowcat fur, but with a similar tensile feline strength. "Able to survive and bloom in harsh conditions. Apparently fragile, fragrant, and lovely, but unstoppable."

"I feel like I've been stopped a few times."

"Not yet. You're still here, still going strong—and climbing higher."

"Why are you being so nice to me?"

"I'm always nice to you."

"No. Sometimes you're grumpy and taciturn." But she smiled as she said it, her tone teasing again. "Like in explaining to me why this place."

"Then I'll explain. There's something I want you to see." He took her gloved hand and tugged her toward the chapel. She dragged her feet, resisting.

"Am I going to hate this?"

"Why would you ask that?"

"Because this thing you want me to see is why you're being all sweet and seductive, I'm thinking."

Her instincts were good ones. Even without sensing his actual thoughts, she'd sussed him out pretty accurately. Or maybe there was more to it. "Are you able to read my mind again?"

"Some," she admitted. Then shrugged, an exasperated movement, pushing her hood back as she did. "To answer your question, I did get something from meditating in the woods. Nothing like what I did before in Bára. Back then I meditated to calm myself, to try to control what I now understand was a constant inpouring of sgath that I had no idea how to manage or channel. This... this is much quieter in a way, like breathing in mist rather than standing under a waterfall."

He ran a hand over her hair. "It sounds easier on you."

"But a much slower way to build power," she pointed out. "And it's power we need and fast, not as slow as this."

"I'm sorry for that. We could—"

She held up a hand to stop him. "Your one for the day—and don't be. We've agreed this is the right course of action. The same course we've been on since you accepted my proposal of marriage. I just need to hold up my end of the deal."

"Next time, I'll propose to you."

She smiled, then squared her shoulders. His tiny warrior. "Show me this thing already and then you can feed me."

"We can eat first," he offered.

She arched her brows. "And delay the fun? Never."

"It won't be *that* bad," he muttered, pulling her along while she was feeling amused at him still.

She balked again at the threshold, peering into the darker hallway. "Will I need Chuffta?"

"I don't think so, but we can leave the door open so you can call him if you do." The derkesthai perched on a log he'd dragged to just in front of and beside the fire, digging his talons into it, perched like a bird of prey. At the moment, he'd swiveled his head backwards on his neck to gaze at Oria while they silently communed.

"All right," she breathed, and gripped his hand more tightly, interlacing her gloved fingers with his. The sensation felt very like actually touching her, with the plush velvet against his skin whetting his anticipation for the rest of the evening.

But first this. *Please, Arill, let this help her.*

The corridor between the cabin and the chapel wasn't long—more a vestibule to allow one or the other to be closed off, depending on whether any guardians lived on site, or if visitors wished to use the chapel in private. The air drafted a bit chilly from the larger building. With its higher ceiling and echoing space, it took longer to heat up. For this reason, the builders had put small fireplaces at intervals along the walls. Lonen had set alight only the one next to the altar. They wouldn't be in here long—he hoped—so he hadn't built it up as much as in the cabin. When Oria shivered and drew the cloak tighter around herself with her free hand, he regretted that choice, then realized her reaction wasn't to the temperature.

Her gaze, the copper flat with shock, was fixed on the retablo over the altar. She saw it, too, what had prompted him to bring his own sorceress to this place.

His memory hadn't failed or misled him—as Oria's astonished reaction confirmed. The woman in the center panel of the retablo looked like her. Looked Báran, rather. And similar to Gallia, a woman from one of Bára's sister-cities, with the high cheekbones, slender build, and fair hair of Oria and Gallia's people. More, she possessed a certain look to her eyes, as if the artist had observed and attempted to capture that glimmer of enchantment he'd so often glimpsed in his own sorceress's gaze.

Oria pulled away, moving closer to the painted wooden panel, and trailed her fingers over the edges, careful not to touch the old gesso. The illustration showed a sorceress of Oria's people, almost certainly. Though the edges of the retablo had crumbled somewhat with age, the gessoed layers of paint flaking away, it seemed clear what she carried in her hand, half hidden in her skirts: the gold mask of her office as priestess, dangling by the ribbons.

"Her hair isn't copper, like yours." His voice came out as a reverent hush, whispering back from the silent stones. "But when I saw you in that window in Bara, you reminded me of her and this place, without my realizing it. I only connected it consciously in Arill's Temple, thinking how the image of the goddess in our family chapel reminded me of you—but this illustration even more so. At first I thought it was only because of the framing, the way the side panels echo the pillars flanking that window you stood in. But then I thought, no, it's more. Ever since that memory hit, I've been trying to reconstruct what she carried, wondering if it could be a mask. It seemed like maybe it could be, though guess I never paid it that much attention. Usually Arill carries a stalk of grain in one hand and a scythe in the other. But this looks like a mask, like yours, the one you had, so that's significant, yes?"

"Yes," she agreed quietly. "This is Arill?"

"Not really. This chapel is dedicated to Arill's worship, but this woman was considered to be one of Arill's priestesses elevated to semi-divine status. An avatar of the goddess." He pointed at the words scrolling in painted text on the side panels. "That's what this bit says."

"It tells her story?" Oria asked in a strangled tone. Maybe he should have waited. Enjoyed their evening together and then shown her in the morning. But that wouldn't have been fair, knowing this was here and keeping it from her.

"It's a short piece in a longer history. It's written in an antiquated script, mostly about the deeds she performed that pleased Arill, so that when she passed on she went to serve in the Hall of Warriors."

"Will you read it to me?"

He cleared his throat. "I am not skilled at reading aloud—"

"I'm looking for information, not entertainment. Just translate the essence of it." Her voice came out taut, her profile sharp with some humming tension.

He focused on the words, letting her interpret the meaning

of them. "When Odymesen returned from the Seven-Year Wars, he and his warriors brought with them many prizes, including fair-haired slave women from desert cities built of gold. As ephemeral as they were beautiful, many of the foreigners did not live long, but languished and eventually perished. The strongest among them, however, Odymesen's favorite, survived many years, bearing him fair-haired sons and bringing him and the Destrye joy and riches beyond their imagining. Beloved of Arill, she loved this place best, so she was laid to rest here, with highest funeral honors."

Oria was silent, contemplating. Then, "What was her name?"

He shook his head slowly, stalling on the inevitable argument. They'd gone round on this subject with his warhorse, somehow ending up with the ignominious moniker of "Buttercup," which was entirely his fault. This would have to go much worse discussing a woman of Oria's people. "It doesn't say."

"Why not? Her name must be recorded somewhere if this whole story is."

"Not if she didn't exactly have one."

Oria slid him a look. "Of course she had a name. You mean that this doesn't say what it was."

"Back in those days, women didn't have names, as such," he hedged. "So there wouldn't have been one to record."

Her copper eyes sparked, reminding him of the glass forges of Bára. "Like animals."

He winced. "An unfortunately accurate parallel."

"Incredible. I can't believe you just admit to it."

"As opposed to what, Oria?" he threw up his hands in exasperation. Nothing like wading directly into an argument you'd hoped to avoid. "I'm not going to lie about it. That's our past. Yes, an abomination, but pretending things weren't that way won't magically make it so that it never happened. The Destrye have a saying that a man who flinches from the shames of the past will never recognize the dark paths that lead back to them."

She punched her fists to her hips. "Fine. But a Báran woman or one from our sister-cities would have had a name."

He shrugged his impotence away. "It wouldn't have occurred to the Destrye then to ask for it or to record it. She was Odymesen's."

Oria ground her teeth at that. "If this place is dedicated to her, what is *it* called?"

He held her gaze, not letting himself look away or step back. "Odymesen'y Chapel. Putting the 'y' at the end of his name denotes his woman. That's why most traditional Destrye female names end with a 'y' sound."

The look she gave him could have frozen fire. "Are they going to write me in the histories as Lonen'y?"

"If so, it would be as an honorific," he suggested, hoping she didn't read in him the primitive thrill of pleasure the sound of that gave him.

"Well it sounds stupid," she hissed. No surprise they wouldn't have like minds on that one. "Never mind all that. What does 'highest funeral honors' mean?"

"It means that she was buried as befits a warrior—and that we believe she entered the Hall of Warriors, where only those Destrye who die in battle are admitted."

Oria blinked, long and slow, that considering veiling of her eyes that never boded well, magical tension coiling palpably around him. His system sprang to alert and, though he'd never draw his battle-axe on her, he stretched his fingers to disperse the instinct to reach for it. "What happens to women otherwise, in this brilliant afterlife," she asked in a lethal tone, "or to children who take ill, or those men not *fortunate* enough to die battle-axe in hand?"

"I don't know why you're mad at me," he replied as calmly and evenly as he could. "I'm only telling you what I was taught. I'm not the enemy here."

That keen sense of attack receded. His response had been instinctive—from the memory of that shimmering sense of lethal danger swirling around her, one he'd learned well in Bára. She was gaining her magic back, slowly or not. An exultant surge of triumph filled him, replacing his previous wariness. Bringing Oria to the chapel had been the right thing to do.

She turned in a circle, reminding him of how she'd done that when they dismounted, eyes closed, her face that serene mask, as if she listened or scented for something. Or reached with some other sense. "Answer my question, please," she said in an absent tone.

He let out a breath of regret. "It depends. Some say they go to serve the warriors in the Hall. Others that they're reborn, in hopes of living a life where they can die a warrior's death. Most think that the souls of those not admitted to the Hall of Warriors go back to the roots of Arill's tree, to provide nutrients."

She cracked an eye open. "You Destrye have serious issues."

"Fine. What do Bárans believe? You have a temple, but I've only heard you reference the moons. I've never heard you swear by any god or goddess. Who do you pray to?"

"Haven't you been paying attention?" She broke into a beatific smile, one that covered sharp teeth. "You're the one who pointed it out. I *am* the goddess—or my ancestress was—

so who do you think the gods pray to?"

He shook his head at her, trying to look stern, but failing in the face of her saucy arrogance. "Do me a favor and don't let my council hear you say that."

"I wouldn't." She closed her eyes again, turning slowly. "I don't really believe that, for the record. If Arill was a sorceress, I'm sure they called her a goddess long after her death. Or this one—I'm going to find out her name, or give her one, as a last resort—she likely only wanted to help. Her Destrye barbarian lover and all his people. We sorceresses are apparently easy prey for that sort of thing."

"Not so easy," he muttered. "Not easy at all."

"What's that?"

"Nothing, love."

Her close-lipped smile deepened, showing the deep dimples in her cheeks on either side. They gave her a girlish, even impish look completely at odds with the questing magic coursing around him. "We don't pray to anyone," she said. "We pay respect to the moons, yes. Sgatha and Grienon, sources of magic, the female and the male, the waxing and waning. Death is the ultimate waning. Like the new moon, a spirit emerges again, a slim crescent that..." her words had fallen into an almost singsong chant and she trailed off, facing a niche set into a wall on the far side of the altar. "Where is her body buried?"

"It would have been burned and the ashes sealed into a vessel. I have to warn you that I won't let you disturb her—"

"I'm not interested in her ashes," Oria cut him off, going to the niche, her eyes closed still.

"What are you doing then?"

"I'm seeing with sgath sight. Physical vision interferes, so it's easier with my eyes closed."

"You do have it back then."

"Some. As I said, it's slow, but getting stronger." She moved her face, reminding him of an animal testing the wind a distant scent. "You're right—it's better here. My ancestress liked it here for a good reason. I just need to find her place."

"Is that what you're looking for?"

"What? No. Her meditation place—where she gathered and hopefully pooled sgath—will be outside somewhere. At least, it's not here in these two buildings or I'd feel it. I'll seek it out in the morning. I knew something called to me, but I wasn't sure what. Right now I'm looking for her mask."

That cursed thing. He'd hated Oria's mask, the way it hid her face from him. More, which he'd admit only in the darkness of his heart, the thing gave him the creeps. "Why do you want it?" he asked, carefully neutral. "It might not even be here."

"If it isn't, what became of it? It's solid gold, so I'd think you'd know if someone had it as a part of their art collection. If they burned her with it—as she would have asked—then it wouldn't have melted, so they'd have had to put it with her ashes. If this Odymesen really loved her—"

"He did." Lonen said it with too much force, startling Oria into turning toward him, though she didn't open her eyes, making him wonder what she saw in him with her sgath sight. "He loved her. No man would go to such trouble if not."

Oria smiled, opening her eyes to shower him with the warmth of her gaze. "This is something I've come to understand."

He shifted his weight, wanting to do something with the powerful emotion she evoked in him—though the impulse at the forefront of his mind involved utterly distracting her from her current task, so he held back, letting her finish whatever she was doing. When he had her attention, he'd command it undivided.

"I'm going to ask you for more trouble, love," she said, gesturing at the stone beneath the niche. "I need you to break that open."

~ 13 ~

S HE HAD TO give him credit. Though her Destrye warrior clearly seethed with impatience, shock at her proposed sacrilege—and with the smoky sense of frustrated lust—he firmed his jaw against whatever argument he longed to throw at her and surveyed the problem.

"Arill forbids grave raiding," he finally ground out.

"Do you think she'll smite you?" Oria almost regretted baiting him when he rounded on her.

"Did I laugh at you when you explained that your dual magical nature was anathema to *your* people?" he demanded. "Even though it makes no Arill-cursed sense when you are clearly all the more powerful for it?"

"Maybe that's why it's anathema," she replied, softly and pointedly. "Maybe our cultures make rules to prevent our worst natures from taking control. You say Arill's taming hand stopped the Destrye wandering and raiding—maybe the injunction against grave-robbing was simply a rule to stop your greedier ancestors from causing more grief by unearthing bodies and ashes simply to get the good stuff they were buried with."

He shook his head at her irreverence, but put his hands on his hips and studied the stone beneath the niche that whispered of the mask behind. It called to her, this ancient object of power. The Báran priests and priestesses didn't talk much about infusing inanimate objects with sgath, but that could be because the cities themselves served that purpose. She'd felt bereft ever since losing hers.

"Why do you want it?" he asked again.

"I'm really not sure. I have a feeling."

"Are you sure this 'feeling' doesn't have something to do with pride, with getting back what they took from you, what you think of as your rightful rank as priestess?"

"It *is* my rightful rank!" she fired back. Lonen gave her a mild look, raising his brows at her vehemence.

"Because his words didn't strike a nerve at all," Chuffta commented from the other room.

"Did I call you?"

"No. That's the beauty of my superior abilities. I can be ready to offer advice and *tend the fire in the other room."*

"Just don't burn the place down because you're distracted by eavesdropping on me," she grumbled at him, and he sent her an affectionate thought, despite her crankiness. The exchange made her take a steadying breath, which her Familiar had no doubt intended.

Lonen had gone back to studying the sepulcher, but with a sense of patient waiting emanating from him. It grounded her in an unexpected way to feel more of his emotional presence, to again catch the edge of a thought. It felt beyond good to have sgath flowing through her, however mildly, to see the world again in the resonances beyond physical sight. She liked the power of it, far better than the weakness of being without. If that made her as power-hungry as her brother, as the worst of the sorcerers and sorceresses of Bára, then so be it. She'd manage somehow.

This is how I'm meant to be. For better or worse, I am this as much as Buttercup is a warhorse and Lonen is a warrior.

"And I am a Bringer of Fire!" Chuffta added an evil cackle.

"I worry about you. I truly do."

"I love you, too," he replied, and she realized he'd fallen into their same habit of using the expression of love as a way of offering forgiveness or appreciation. Which she supposed it was. And if anything could save her from becoming like her aunt Tania—whatever it was that she had done—then Lonen's love, even in the form of nagging reminders about her prideful ways, would be it.

"I understand your point," she said to Lonen, "and I agree it's valid for you to caution me." There. That sounded very adult and reasonable.

"Chuffta agreed with me, did he?" Lonen didn't look at her, instead squatting to examine the stonework more closely, running his fingertips along the mortar between, but his lips twitched suspiciously.

"Fine. Laugh. Yes, he did. But, Lonen—" She moved into the edge of his vision, which brought her closer to the niche. The mask was there. Oh yes. Calling to her. "You know that before I left Bára I was but a newly made priestess, so there's a great deal I never learned. Still, something in me is certain that the masks are more than a demonstration that we can see without physical eyes. The masks are too solidly a part of the practice of sorcery. Why would they have been so determined to take my mask away for my magical crimes, if not to hamper me in practicing it?"

Lonen glanced up at her, nodded crisply. "Makes sense. I think I can get it out of there." He stood, uncoiling in his smooth strength, and took her hand, turning her back toward the cabin.

"Do you need certain tools?" she asked, confused.

He let go her hand and snaked his arm around her waist under the cloak. "Tools will help, yes, but I'm also waiting until morning to attack this test my sorceress wife has set me."

"It's not a test," she retorted.

"In the stories, the witch always sets challenges for the hero to overcome before he can claim the beautiful princess. In my case, I happen to have both in one. And I intend to enjoy my wife this evening, while I have her all to myself."

"If we're going by the stories, then you shouldn't get to enjoy the reward before you successfully complete the test."

"Good thing this isn't a story then."

"Yes, because I'm not a witch."

He snugged her against him, shutting the door to the drafty chapel. "Neither are you a princess, my queen."

HE'D SET THE stage for romance, which made her feel unaccountably shy. They'd truly done so little together sexually, though the enforced intimacy of travel, injury, and illness had made them familiar with each other's bodies in a way she'd never expected before her wedding. She'd had a naïve young woman's ideas about marriage—mostly about high-minded ideals and a sort of silk-draped, candlelit cleanness to it all.

Though little of her marriage to Lonen had worked out that way, he seemed to have read *her* mind and created something of that romantic ideal in the little cabin. The inviting bed spoke volumes, along with the candles burning softly. The table for two, with wine waiting. The delicately scented blossoms.

Lonen turned her, smoothing his hands over the fur cloak. "Are you warm enough to take this off?"

She nodded, unable to speak around her suddenly thick tongue. One day she'd feel easy and natural with this man, but that day had not yet come. With his gray eyes intent on hers, he undid the fastening, taking the cloak away. Though she still wore her layers of skirts and fur-lined gown, she shivered a little, feeling naked.

"Would it be easier to eat without the gloves?" he asked.

It would be, so she stripped them off, too, putting them into his expectant hand. He took them over to the bed, setting them on a table next to it—and next to several other things she couldn't quite make out. He caught her curious look. "You'll need them later," he said, with that cheerfully lustful grin that warmed her as if he'd caressed her between her legs.

"I'm going to keep Buttercup company," Chuffta said. *"Don't let the fire burn down because you're all distracted frolicking with your mate."*

"You don't have to go. It's cold out there."

"Buttercup lets me sleep on his back—he's very warm. And you need privacy." Chuffta flew up to Lonen and hovered expectantly.

"Thanks, man," Lonen said, not arguing in the least. "I'll let him into the stable. Go ahead and sit, pour us some wine."

His brief absence gave her a moment to gather herself. She trusted Lonen utterly. When he'd pleasured her to consummate their wedding, he'd been exceptionally careful not to touch her skin. In fact, the lengths he'd gone to—and the sexually scandalous game he'd constructed around it—made her face go hot at the memory. As did her behavior at the oasis when she'd tried to seduce him and he'd refused her, for her own good. He no doubt had something in mind for tonight to let them safely enjoy each other. She let herself relax. Enough with fretting.

Anticipation, however, only warmed her further.

The door opened and Lonen returned, bringing a cloud of icy fresh air with him that helped cool her cheeks. Still, she kept her face studiously averted, lest he glimpse too much of her salacious thoughts—she wasn't *that* relaxed—and belatedly poured the wine into the hammered metal cups. If she ever made it back to Bára or one of her sister-cities, she'd bring back a case of glasses. Wine didn't taste the same drunk from metal or wood.

Lonen sat, giving her an opaque look, then lifted his mug in a toast. "To my beautiful witch-queen—may I never fail in the challenges she sets me."

"I'm not drinking to that," she said on a laugh.

He made a mournful face. "You wish me to fail?"

"I'm not a witch and I'm not testing you."

"No? Let's see how I do anyway." He retrieved something from the fire, putting on a pair of leather gloves to carry it, then set it on the table, removing the metal lid to display the contents. The scent of rich broth, roasted vegetables and cream rose out of it, and she lifted her gaze to his expectant one in delight.

"How did you do this?"

"Baeltya had the cooks assemble several casseroles like this and set them outside to freeze. We need simply warm them in a fire. Can't let you backslide in regaining those gorgeous curves."

She wrinkled her nose at him, but accepted the generous helping and dug in. "What about you? Don't you need meat to rebuild those mighty thews?"

He grinned easily, ladled still more onto her plate, then fetched another metal container from the fire, opening it to release a meaty aroma. "Baeltya made her plans for me, too."

"We're well taken care of, then."

Comfortable silence settled between them as they dug into their respective meals, the delicious flavor and welcome nourishment of the hot meal hitting her stomach making her voraciously hungry. Snacking as they rode had felt satisfying enough, but nothing like this. Lonen kept dishing more onto her plate until she sat back, groaning as she realized she'd eaten the entire thing. She splayed her hands over her distended belly. "I can't believe I ate so much."

Lonen eyed her with amusement, using the last slice of the warmed bread they'd shared to soak up the last juices of his. "Don't pretend you have anything like a pot belly. I'll be happy if I can get you out of concave."

"You'll see plenty of belly on me if I get pregnant," she retorted.

He went still. Then set his utensils aside, laced his fingers together, and propped his chin on them, gray eyes both grave and cautiously alight. "Is that a possibility?" he asked in a careful tone.

She tried not to blush, she really did, but to no avail. Still, the excitement of her realization in the chapel made it relatively easy to overcome any shyness at such a frank conversation with him. "Maybe so."

"Because you warned me, when we agreed to this marriage, that you would never bear me heirs."

"That was when I thought we'd never be able to have sex of any kind, and you've found plenty of ways around that."

His grin went wolfish. "I did warn you," he pointed out.

"You did," she agreed, feeling somewhat wolfish in kind.

Him, wending into her. Or perhaps all herself, and her desire for him. "And since you've ably demonstrated your inventiveness in that arena, then I feel compelled to point out that Odymesen and his sorceress managed the deed. 'Bore him many fair-haired sons.' I assume she provided the world with a few daughters as well, and they simply weren't worth mentioning."

Lonen was staring at her, thunderstruck.

"Didn't catch that, did you?" Being the one to tell him gave her a decided thrill. Happy news for a change. "That's the problem with you barbarians. You're always focusing on—" she broke off with a little shriek when he pounced on her, lifting her out of the chair and carrying her to the bed.

"You were saying?" he asked politely, rapidly undoing the fastenings of her gown.

"I—I've forgotten," she stammered, losing the thought entirely as the fur-lined velvet parted, exposing her breasts, the nipples hardening almost painfully at the sudden chill.

Lonen's eyes were hot, gone silver with lust when he lifted them to her face. "Cold?"

"Not enough to cover up." She wanted this. Wanted his gaze on her and more.

"Good. Take that off." He reached for her gloves on the table, watching her as she shrugged out of the upper part of the gown, pulling her arms out of the tight sleeves, then pushing the whole thing down to puddle at her feet. He raised a brow at the petticoat layers still belling around her. "How many of those do you have on?"

"A lot. I lost count," she admitted. "But I was warm."

"Put these on and turn around." He handed her the velvet gloves again, then began untying her underskirts one by one when she did as he bade.

"I love it when you get all bossy," she teased him but it came out breathless, especially as the last of her underthings came off to his yanking, leaving her naked but for the tall boots and the elbow-length scarlet gloves.

"I know you do," he answered, in all seriousness, his voice throaty. "Bend over and put your hands on the bed."

She did, then gasped as his hands—cool and a little rough— ran over her bottom and then up her waist and belly to grasp her breasts. Looking down, she saw he'd donned gloves similar to hers, but made of thin leather. He snugged his groin against her rear, his erection pressing neatly into the cleft of her buttocks, rocking there.

"Is this all right?" he asked in her ear. Still dressed, he pressed his body all along hers, one hand massaging her breast, the other sliding down her belly, pushing against her mons.

"Yes," she breathed. It was working. She received a lot of input from him this way, but not the overwhelming kind from skin-to-skin contact. His exuberance, that simmering male arousal and strength filled her empty spaces, dizzying her. "It's good," she murmured, indulging in shimmying against his grip. "Another test passed."

"I'm so glad to hear it, witch," he growled. "Now spread those pretty thighs for me."

"I'm not a—" She squealed when he slapped her bottom, hard enough to sting. Perversely it made her sex heat that much more and she spread her thighs on a moan—dropping her head when his gloved hand dove into the opening, dragging through her slick tissues with nerve-shattering results.

"That's a good girl," he crooned in her ear, grinding his hard cock through his leather pants against her cleft again. "You're just a tame witch, aren't you? My tame witch."

"I'm not a—" She cried out and shuddered when his gloved

fingers pinched her nipple.

"Admit it," he demanded. "You're mine. My tame witch." His other hand stroked between her legs, making her frantic.

"Yes," she nearly sobbed. "I'm your tame witch."

"Because you need this from me," he gentled his touch, teasing her nipple now, pushing the tip of a gloved finger inside her. The fever pitch of her arousal only intensified.

"I do. Oh, Lonen, please."

"I like it when you beg." He sounded all satisfied male. "You'll be doing a lot of that. Lie back on the bed and spread your legs for me."

"My boots and…"

"I like them. Leave them on. In fact…" He walked away, then came back. "You can stand up and face me."

With some chagrin, she realized she'd remained where he'd last positioned her, and stood up, her face hot. With a quirk of a smile he draped the shadowcat cloak over her shoulders, fastening it again at her throat and bidding her to lift her hair out so it streamed down the back. The cloud of soft fur teased all along her skin, another stimulation. Lonen ran his gloved hands over her, stopping to tease her nipples, stroking the skin of her thighs above the furry stockings, dipping finger into her aching sex.

"Your skin is a white like this fur," he murmured. "Except for this pink." He tweaked a nipple so she squirmed. "And this copper." He cupped her mons with his hand, lifting her to her toes, so she grabbed ahold of his shoulders. It brought them nearly nose to nose, his breath mingling with hers, hot silver eyes boring into hers. "My prize. My tame, captive witch."

"I want to touch you, too," she got out rocking her hips against his hand. "My warrior king."

"Then do it. Touch me. Tend to me." He let her down,

leaving her sex empty and wanting. So she hurried to undress him, dropping his clothes to the floor in her haste, but taking the time to run her hands over his shoulders and chest muscles, down the flat of his abdomen, the velvet of her gloves snagging the whorls of hair. Standing again on her tiptoes—Lonen's hands going to her waist to steady her—she reached behind his neck to pull the leather tie from his hair. When she went to toss it aside, he stopped her, taking it from her and setting it carefully on the bedside table.

"It's the one you saved for me, in Bára, after I left," he said, as if explaining.

"That didn't mean anything..." She trailed off at the look he gave her, possessive and pleased.

"It did. It meant you thought about me like I thought about you." He wound a hand in her hair, tugging her head back, gently and remorselessly, so she had to look into his face. He trailed a gloved finger over her lips, his eyes following the movement. She smelled her own musky arousal on it. "It meant you wanted me, and waited for me to return."

She nearly protested, but that was all true. Though it had seemed unlikely that she'd ever see him again, even impossible, she'd kept the tie, dreaming over how he'd felt in her mind, and maybe fantasizing a little about her Destrye warrior.

His face tightened, reading something of that in hers. "Finish undressing me, witch."

Desire coiling hard in her again, she knelt to pull off his boots, then unfastened and tugged down his leather pants, helping him step out of them. His cock, freed, stood out from its deeper nest of hair, and she took a moment to study that part of him. From this angle his man jewels were more visible, hanging full and turgid beneath. Hesitant, she glanced up, to find him watching her with heavy-lidded, slumberous silver eyes.

"Go ahead," he told her, not playing his games, stroking a hand over her hair. The leather made it crackle like fire. "Explore, if you like."

"Spread your legs," she told him, smiling to herself when he obliged. Cupping his balls, she weighed them, fascinated by the way the firm insides, like eggs, moved inside the looser outer skin. Lonen groaned, hand tightening in her hair. "Does that hurt?" she asked.

"No. It's good. So good. Touch me, love."

So, she kept one hand holding his jewels, cupping and massaging them, taking his cock in the other, stroking the velvet over his shaft so it went smooth in one direction, against the nap in the other. Both made him groan and shudder in turn.

"Enough," he gasped, urging to her feet and pushing her back onto the bed. "Spread your legs for me, as I told you."

She did, with not even an inkling of refusing him. There was a power in this, too, lying back on her fur cloak and parting her thighs for his avid gaze. He grasped her knees, pushing them wider apart and back. "This is pink, too," he told her. "Blushing for me like you do when you think about having me."

Of course, she blushed at that, that he read her so easily. An irony that she could feel shyness over that when she was so totally physically exposed.

"Hold your knees apart for me like that, so I don't accidentally touch you," he instructed, putting one knee on the bed and stroking the now wet and rougher leather down the tender skin of the inside of her thighs. His cock bobbed over her, enticing, and she wished she could put her mouth on it, or put him inside her.

"Why do you get leather gloves and I get velvet?" Her breaths came in pants as he toyed with her, brushing his fingers along the outside of her burning core, not quite where she needed it most.

His fierce silvery gaze lifted to hers, his hair loose now, snaking in curls around his strong shoulders. "You can have leather. I'll wear velvet. I'll have gloves made for us both in every fabric imaginable, so we can torment each other with the textures." He pushed a finger, made thicker by the glove, inside her. "How's this one?"

She couldn't answer, her eyes rolling back in her head, her breath stolen away. The invasion penetrated deeper than the physical, all of him coming into her. Having his finger, even gloved, inside her body permeated her with his particular energy, that core vibrance that had drawn her from the first moment.

He slid the finger in and out of her, mimicking the intercourse they couldn't have, and she lifted her hips in answer thrusts. "Yes?" he asked, a purr in his voice saying he knew the answer.

"Yes," she panted. "More."

"More," he echoed, working a second finger inside her. It stretched her, the pleasurable ache making her keen. "Look at me," Lonen commanded and she opened her eyes. He'd moved so he hovered over her, bracing himself on an elbow next to her head, a breath away from laying himself on her. Below, beyond the plank of his body, his fingers thrust in and out of her, diligently building the fire within. But all she could see was his face, so close to hers, his gaze mirroring the love and desire that radiated through her, from his touch inside her and wafting off his skin along with his intense body heat. Consciously or not, he undulated with her, moving as she did, and she could almost believe he made love to her in truth.

She reached down and took his cock in her velvet grasp. His mouth fell open slightly, his face taking on a strained mien. Fingers thrusting harder, the hilt of his hand slamming against her, knuckle rubbing her pearl of pleasure, pressure building. Building.

With a crash and a scream, she orgasmed, funneling her convulsion into her grip on his cock, angling it toward her entrance.

"Oria…" Lonen gasped, straining to pull his hips back. "Love—"

"Yes," she demanded, working him faster.

He went rigid, neck arching back and face suffusing with blood, a guttural roar erupting from his throat. Liquid splashed against her entrance—she hoped. Between his thrusting fingers and her own copious juices, she couldn't be sure, but he knew. Veins bulging in his temples beside bright sliver eyes, he worked himself in her hand, echoing the movement with his fingers.

"This is my cock," he whispered, as he had on their wedding night. "Planting my seed in your fertile soil. My wife. My lovely sorceress. My queen."

With a fervent wish, she took him in. All of him, savoring and tucking it away, as she had with the forest breath. Keeping it safe. With any luck they'd made a child.

Arill make it so.

<h1 style="text-align:center">~ 14 ~</h1>

H E MADE LOVE to his wife twice more, until she fell into a deep sleep after the third round. All of her moods enchanted him. Submissive, queenly, angry, sweet, passionate, powerful, gasping and begging, fiercely demanding—he loved it all. From sleekly gorgeous, her slim, pale nakedness framed by the fur cloak, ribboned socks, boots and those Arill-forsaken scarlet gloves, to sleepy-eyed and rumpled, hair tousled from sex and sleep, every face of his personal goddess ruled his heart.

Putting his seed inside her, even if only by close proxy, had given him such a powerful rush. Totally unexpected. Absolutely transporting. He couldn't get enough of her.

He had big plans for another session in the morning when she'd recovered—which quickly ground to a halt. Because of him, not her. Though his cock was ready enough, when Oria pulled on a glove to grasp it, he swore viciously, knocking her hand away.

She blinked at him, puzzled and a little hurt. "What's wrong?"

Sitting back on his heels, he examined himself. Erect, yes, but also nearly as crimson as Oria's gloves. His cock glowed with more than aroused color. The entire shaft looked rubbed raw, the head bloodred. Now that her velvet grasp had awakened the nerves, his entire cock throbbed with agony. Not at all a smart thing to do. Good thing his brothers would never know, or he'd hear about this until his deathbed.

Oria raised dubious eyes to his, giving him a weak smile that became a grimace. "Too much chafing?"

Gritting his teeth, he nodded. Really stupid. And inconsiderate. "How about you—are you sore?"

Experimentally she pressed her thighs together, then shrugged a little. "Slightly. In a lovely way. I'll probably walk funny." She blushed as she made the joke, as if she hadn't panted and begged and screamed her pleasure, encouraging him to penetrate every part of her. "I think I had more…lubrication."

Of course she had. Arill shouldn't let his seed take root. He didn't deserve to reproduce.

Oria bit her lip in sympathy. Then he realized it was to keep from laughing. He scowled at her. "Laugh even a little and I'm flipping you over and spanking your bottom until it's the same color as my cock."

With an amazing amount of control, she swallowed every hint of amusement, her face smoothing into a serene mask. Never forget her ability to assume an emotionless demeanor. She sat up, clutching the furs to her breast. "Perhaps some salve of some sort?" she suggested with polite reserve.

The thought of *that* potential burn made him choke. "I'll take care of it."

"I could—"

"It's my cock," he snapped. "I'll handle it."

"I'm sure you will," she murmured as he yanked his shirt over his head, and he thought he detected a ripple of laughter in her voice, but when he whirled on her, she looked as demure as ever. The leather pants scraped his still-engorged cock abominably and he was hard pressed to keep from cursing further, willing the thing to subside already.

"I'm going to check on Buttercup and rescue Chuffta," he said. After the door slammed shut, a peal of laughter rang out, silvery magic riding it like frost on a mountain breeze.

Nice to know he could make his sorceress break *hwil* and laugh—even at his expense.

He stopped to make water on the way back, which turned out to be its own special nightmare. Worth it though. He shook his head at himself. What a night. He'd figure out something for the next time. Smooth leather gloves for her hands, maybe. And oil.

Lots of oil.

Setting those thoughts firmly aside, as they did *not* help with easing his arousal, he went back in to find Oria had already sponge-bathed with water warmed by the fire, and she had nearly finished adding all forty-seven layers of clothing. Why she didn't melt inside all of that, he didn't know, but the flushed and happy expression on her face—along with the sated and sensual smile she greeted him with—spoke volumes.

He could live his whole life happily this way—warm, passionate nights, mornings with laughter. Get through all of this and they would. He would make it happen.

Holding up the tools he'd brought from the extra packs stowed with Buttercup, he pointed to the chapel. "I'm going to do your grave-robbing. If Arill smites me, you'll have to get off the mountain on your own."

She nodded, giving him a serious look, though her eyes sparkled. "I'll stand ready to bargain for your immortal soul." Exchanging a thought with Chuffta, who lolled belly-up in front of the blazing fire, she lost the smirk and added, "Try not to touch the mask though, if you can help it."

He turned back. "Why not? I touched your mask, back in Bára."

She picked up his hair tie and went to him, bidding him to turn around. Gathering his loose curls together—which in truth he'd forgotten about—she tied it back for him. "I don't know," she finally said, a remote sound to her voice. "A feeling I have. Chuffta thinks so, too."

"Someone would have had to touch it to inter it with her ashes," he pointed out.

"Still." She went to get her cloak. "Why take the chance?"

"You're the sorceress. I'm just the muscle." He opened the door and entered the dark and considerably chillier chapel. Oria followed behind, bringing a lantern from the cabin. "I'd light the fire, but this shouldn't take long."

She nodded, shivering and drawing the cloak tighter around her, casting a long and pensive look at the retablo of her ancestress. "I wonder what happened to her children," she said, as he began chipping at the loosest part of the mortar at the top.

With any luck the cover stones would come free and they could extract the mask without further disturbing the ashes. Oria might like to tease him and imply that he was superstitious, but why risk angering the goddess? *Why take the chance?* Oria had said. Each of them with their own talismans for dealing with unknown powers.

"I imagine they lived out their lives," he answered.

"But wouldn't they have had a sensitivity to magic, being her get?"

"No temple to train them, though." The mortar gave a little, but not as easily as he'd hoped.

"That would be even worse. The magic comes to you anyway—and makes you kind of crazy if you don't know how to deal with it."

"Well, then they probably didn't survive long among the Destrye. I can vouch that crazy people are barely tolerated now—back then would have been much worse. They'd have been exposed to the elements as babes or young children, or left behind if the tribe moved. If they made it to adulthood, the boys would have died in duels and the girls killed by angry husbands. And that's only if the families managed to marry them off." With a grunt, he applied more leverage, and the capstone grated free. "Got it!"

The thing was heavy so he skewed it to the side, hoping to avoid lifting it off entirely. "Bring the candle here and see if—" He broke off, seeing Oria's face streaming with tears. "What? What happened? Did..." Oh.

She wiped the tears away with an impatient hand, bringing the candle closer. "Don't mind me. I'm just emotional for some reason. Being here, in her tomb, where she was buried so far from home among a people who didn't even give her a name. And then thinking of her children, killed so ruthlessly, because of something they couldn't control..."

He took the candle and set it down. His idiocy record for the morning continued in full strength. Putting his hand over hers where it rested on her belly—had she been aware of the gesture?—he ran his other over her shining hair, once again brushed smooth. "Speculation only. And that won't happen to you or our children. You have a name and I'll make sure all of Dru—and Bára—knows forever of the mighty Sorceress Queen Oria of the Destrye. Our children will be protected and blessed by both Arill and the magic you'll bring them. They'll grow up to be kings and queens in their own right. Maybe one in charge of every one of your sister-cities."

She laughed, a little watery. "Ever the optimist."

"That's right." He cupped the back of her head and kissed her hair just over her forehead. As much as he regretted her unhappiness, it also moved him a great deal that she already felt so deeply for their future children. The way she held her hand so protectively over her belly… well, it seemed women sometimes knew these things instinctively. Perhaps they'd made a baby last night. A child conceived in this sacred place, where warrior and sorceress had joined before, would have to be specially blessed.

"I should have told you," he said, waiting for her to look up at him, copper eyes dark with tears. He pointed with his chin to the opposite wall. "Odymesen's ashes are interred here, too. This isn't just her place, but their place. I don't know if it helps to know it, but she was never alone."

A smile trembled into place on her lips. "It helps."

"Good. Now come fetch your treasure."

Her eyes widened. "It's in there?"

"Of course it is. You knew it all along." The gleam of gold hadn't surprised him in the least.

"I guessed."

"Uh huh."

She wrinkled her nose at him, which made him happy to see her saucy again. Taking the candle over to the sepulcher, she leaned over and peered in. A long breath sighed out of her. "It is in there."

"On a tile like you had in Bára for yours, I think." He looked over her shoulder, the mask now clearly illuminated in the niche built for it. "Her ashes are sealed beneath, I suspect, so you'll be relieved to know there should be no smiting imminent."

"I am beyond relieved," she said in a dry tone. "Will you hold this?"

SHE HANDED HIM the candle, noting the tightness around his eyes. For all his joking, Lonen harbored concerns about this project still. More than his dislike of her old mask. But he'd set aside his apprehensions and helped her do what she asked of him.

And there it was. Radiating old power, hot as the sun on her face. Lonen might not have doubted what they'd find, but she hadn't been certain of what she perceived. With sgath sight, the thing didn't look like a mask at all. It reminded her of how the Trom appeared on that other plain, like black suns radiating a kind of non-light. Not moonlight, not sunlight, but something the reverse of both.

The dreams came back to her, Chuffta's eyes going matte black, as if they absorbed light instead of reflecting it. Yar's eyes, looking like that after he summoned the Trom. *You've taken not one, but several steps farther down your path,* the Trom had said to her. Was this another of those steps? She shuddered with more than cold.

But the course hadn't changed. Lonen and the Destrye needed her. The Bárans back home, laboring under Yar's deranged regime needed her. Food, water, safety—all of that called for magic, and a great deal of it. Did she dare attempt to wrestle these ancient magics?

"I need you," she called to Chuffta and he winged in, landing on her shoulder. *"What do you think of this?"*

He snaked his head around, angling it from side to side, peering at the artifact with brilliant green eyes. *"It looks like any*

Báran mask to me."

"Do you think it's safe for me to take it?"

"I think you have to." His mind-voice sounded unusually somber.

"Why?"

"Because you feel it. There's a reason you wanted Lonen to dig it out. A reason it called to you."

"I don't know what the reason is though. And… it could be more than I can handle."

"We shall no doubt find out." Now he lifted his head, looking at her. His long tail slipped up her sleeve, finding a spot of skin above the glove, coiling around, infusing her with his cool, dry presence. *"Go on, take it. I'm ready."*

"Here we go," she said aloud. Lonen unstrapped his battle-axe, holding it at the ready.

He shrugged a little self-consciously when she raised her eyebrows at him. "Can't hurt, right?" he said.

Her barbarian, ever ready to protect her, even from the unseen. Reaching in with her gloved hands, she took up the mask. Heavier than hers had been, the thing sang of the weight of centuries. What must have been ribbons crumbled away into dust as she lifted it out of its niche. The candlelight caught the gold, the flicker of shadows on the subtle molding of the eyeless mask giving the illusion of a face.

For a startled moment, she thought it smiled at her. Then it subsided, losing the momentary illusion of animation and becoming simply a mask again. Very old, very heavy, but only that.

Mostly. In the back of her heart, a soundless tune hummed. A chime, like the breathing of the forest or the chime of the stars dancing together at the oasis. She strained to hear it better, but it retreated, like a memory from childhood she couldn't quite reconstruct.

Holding the mask in one hand, she nipped at her glove with her teeth, drawing it off and letting it fall to the floor where it lay on the chill gray stones like the discarded skin of a scarlet snake. Hovering her fingers over the metal, the sense of radiation from it sang louder. Dragons roaring far away. A distant silhouette of wings. A bloom of fire. More. But not enough. She drew in a deep breath, reaching for all her *hwil*, bracing for the impact.

"Oria, love." Lonen gripped her shoulder, tense concern flooding into her. "Don't rush things. There's time for you to study it."

She gazed up at him, that craggy, scarred face, hard and yet tender. So beloved in such a short time. Time and time and time. "There isn't."

And she laid her bare hand on the mask.

~ 15 ~

THE MAGIC GRABBED at her, hard. Rather than a geyser, it yanked her under, the waters of the oasis closing over her head, crushing the breath from her lungs.

No—filling her lungs with water. Which should have drowned her but… then she could breathe it. It swelled in and out of her, her chest like a larger heart, beating the fluid in and out. Sustaining. Nourishing.

Oddly it reminded her of that dream again, of the fire burning her throat, and Chuffta saying it didn't really do that.

"I'm here. And yes. Same, but different."

She tried to frame a reply, but couldn't. Her mind-voice didn't work underwater. Only it wasn't water, it was sgath. A more viscous sgath, purified, but intense. So much. She worked harder to breathe it out again. Couldn't.

"Oria?"

"Oria!"

She opened her eyes and gasped, air burning into her lungs. Lonen's face loomed above hers, echoing on several levels of physical and sgath sight. Waking her from another nightmare? No—the clatter of the gold mask against stone still rang in the air, a harsh bell of warning, a tantalizing chime of waltzing stars.

"I'm here." She drew in more air as slowly as she could,

using the physical discipline to focus on pulling *hwil* into place, shutting down all but physical sight. That steadied the world. "I'm fine."

Lonen's mouth firmed into a harsh line. He gripped her, and she realized she lay on the floor, half in his embrace. "I would greatly prefer," he began in a ragged voice that was nearly a shout, then paused to calm himself. "If you could not do the stopping breathing thing anymore. That would be much better for my continued sanity."

She reached up to touch his face, diverting her fingers to stroke his silky beard when she realized that was the naked hand. "I'll see what I can do."

"Yes." He took a deep breath, let it out, then offered a crooked smile. "Well?"

"She pooled sgath, all right." She struggled to sit up and his arms tightened briefly before he let her go with a sharp shake of his head. Not for her, but for himself.

"Here?" he asked, giving the floor a suspicious look, his fingers twitching for the battle-axe lying next to them. Even discarding it in haste, he kept it near.

"Not exactly, but nearby. It's hard to tell because there's a lot of it and it's very old. Like it's sat and … grown solid over time. Does that make sense?"

Lonen gave her an incredulous look. "Seriously? No. None of this makes sense to me, but I'll take your word for it. The mask?"

"Connected me to it, yes. I'll have to think about how to work with it. Instead of being like drinking from the geyser below Bára, or breathing the mist of the forest, this felt like inhaling stone."

He frowned over her shoulder—in the direction of the mask he'd dashed out of her hands, she realized. "That can't be good for you. We'll put it back for now."

"No." She pushed to her feet, finding her legs weak. With a resigned sigh, Lonen stood, too, helping her up with a hand under her elbow. "Where's Chuffta?"

"Here." His mind-voice sounded strange, and she turned even as Lonen pointed.

Her Familiar perched next to the mask, one talon hooked in a hole where the ribbons would be tied. *"Are you all right?"* she asked him, wondering as she did if she'd ever asked him that before.

"Yes. No. I don't know. I feel strange."

"Strange how?"

"Like I want to be bigger. Much bigger."

ORIA EVENTUALLY AGREED to let Lonen be the custodian of the mask. The fact that she didn't want to give it to him—and that Chuffta showed a similar reluctance to part company with the Arill-cursed thing—finally convinced her of the wisdom of it.

Left to his own devices, he would have sealed it back in its crypt. But Oria refused to even consider it. Her fervor, and the fiery burn in Chuffta's gaze, made it clear he'd have a battle on his hands if he insisted.

And Oria shone with magic again, her hair lifting as she moved, swirling in the unseen currents, her skin as radiant and shimmering as when he first glimpsed her. When she paused to draw her glove back on, the saint in the retablo seemed to gaze over her shoulder, the resemblance so uncanny they could have been sisters.

He handled the mask himself only with gloved hands, wrapping it in layers of leather and tying knots in the ties that bound it. Under the close watch of Oria and Chuffta, he buried the thing at the bottom of the saddlebags. If Buttercup danced sideways when he added the packs to the warhorse's back, that surely had to be because the steed was restive from being cooped up.

Oria would know if there was any reason to fear. And she would tell him. He glanced at her, the remote cool of her face, her gaze drawn inward, contemplating.

"Oria."

Her bright copper eyes, molten with magic, lifted to his when he spoke her name.

"I want you to promise me you won't use the mask without me present."

A line drew in between her brows. "I might need solitude."

"Then we'll figure it out, but no going behind my back on this. You or Chuffta."

She cast her gaze down, her cheeks pinking, revealing that she'd considered it. "Lonen, I—"

He gripped her shoulders, forcing her to look at him, her expression no longer serene, but cagey and assessing. "I mean it. If I have to be a brute of a barbarian about this, I will. But I'll have your promise on this."

Copper fire snapped at him, his skin tingling with the seething static of magic building like a summer storm in a densely hot afternoon. The kind that produced lightning and no rain. And blazes that devoured forests. "Oria, love, listen to me. You know I'm right."

She firmed her lips in mutiny, then the fire fogged and she cast a glance at Chuffta, perched on Buttercup's saddle. Huffing out a breath between pursed lips, she closed her eyes briefly, a sweep of lashes and gone, then smiled at him, her gaze once again more herself. Abruptly he remembered that dream in her bed, that first night he slept with her, when her eyes had turned Trom black.

The hairs lifted on his neck.

"You're right," she was saying, and he shook off the memory. Or was it premonition? "You have my promise. Neither Chuffta nor I will touch the mask without you. You are its keeper and…." She moved into him, wrapping her arms around his waist, burrowing against his chest. "It frightens me, Lonen." Her voice came soft and muffled.

He cupped her head in his hand, using the other to pull his cloak around her, though she hardly needed more warmth. "It frightens me, too," he admitted. "Let's leave it here."

"No." She raised her face, leaning into his hand. "We need it."

"We can find another—"

"Not 'we' as in you and me. We as in Bára, and Dru. Something here started long ago and we're simply picking up the threads of it. Even if we leave the mask here, the course is set. Can't you feel it?"

He could. He didn't much like it, either.

Her gaze went up to the peaks over his shoulder. "So, we ride on and up. And I'll practice with Tania's sgath along the way."

"Tania?"

"My long-lost aunt. I've decided to give her name to my ancestress-of-the-chapel."

"Is that wise?" The feeling of premonition still sat heavy on him.

Oria gave him a look. "I am *not* calling her Odymesen'y."

"I understand, but perhaps a different name…"

"Why—what objection do you have?" She gave no hint of what, but something about her wide eyes made him think she kept them deliberately guileless.

"I think there's something you're not telling me."

She laughed, the magic glinting through it, seeming to manifest in the air like crystals to shower to the ground. No, it had begun to snow. That's all it was.

"Come on, Destrye." She tugged him toward the horse. "Let's go see this lake and talk your mother into sponsoring this wedding you want so badly. And I'll tell you the little I know about my aunt Tania."

Chuffta took off as he lifted her into the saddle, white wings etched against the wintery sky. Oria lifted a crimson-gloved hand to her Familiar and he nipped at her fingers as he flew past. When she transferred her gaze to Lonen, as he settled behind her, she smiled with affection, dropping the hand to caress his cheek.

"It will all be fine," she murmured. "Trust me."

He did. But he held her close, and sent a prayer to Arill to hold them in her hand.

Thank you for reading! I hope you loved the continuing adventures of Oria and Lonen—and Chuffta! The next book in the Sorcerous Moons series is *Oria's Enchantment*. Now that Oria is coming into her true powers, will she be able to resist the dark temptation to use them?

"I can't get enough of Oria and Lonen. Each installment leaves me with a book hangover."

~Kindle Customer

I appreciate your help in spreading the word about my books, including telling a friend or leaving a review. Reviews help readers find books! I'd love it if you'd leave a review on your favorite site.

SIGN UP FOR JEFFE KENNEDY'S NEWSLETTER for fun giveaways from Jeffe and other authors.
landing.mailerlite.com/webforms/landing/r2y4b9

Turn the page for a short excerpt from *Oria's Enchantment*.

~ 1 ~

THE MASK HUNG in her awareness like a blinding sun, scorching bright and enticingly hot. Not that the wintry mountain air made her all that cold. Her husband, Lonen, had gone to great lengths to make sure she stayed warm. No, this was like a physical craving. Oria thirsted for more of the golden mask's rich magic, starving for another taste.

With every stride of Lonen's warhorse, Buttercup, with every minute since that morning when she'd held the artifact in her hands, swept under by its immense power, she missed it exponentially more.

Naturally, she wouldn't tell Lonen.

It wouldn't help anything for him to know how deeply the mask affected her. She'd admitted to being frightened by it and that unwise admission had been more than enough. Freshly shaken from the encounter, she'd promised Lonen she wouldn't use the mask by herself. "Fear," however, didn't accurately describe her emotions.

"Greed" would be a better word—and now she deeply regretted that hasty promise. She wanted the mask with a longing unlike anything she'd felt before, except for perhaps during sexplay with Lonen. He had a way of stoking overpowering need in her. Perhaps if they could have actual intercourse, with skin-to-skin contact, that driving desire might be slaked. As it was, despite his inventive alternatives—or, more likely, entirely as a result of those frustrating games of his—their sexual interludes drove all rational sense from her mind, until she could think of nothing but begging for more and more and more.

She wanted the mask like that—but no amount of begging Lonen would work in this case. She had to find another way.

Even now, riding in the cradle of Lonen's arm, cozy in the shadowcat fur cloak, with the startling peaks of the snow-capped mountains rising against the jewel-bright blue sky, she couldn't rest content. The mask mentally tugged at her. After the session with it in the chapel, Lonen had taken the mask from her, holding it suspiciously in gloved hands—and keeping it out of hers. All because she'd lost a bit of time while communing with it, and felt a little ill and disoriented after-ward. He flatly refused to give it back, too, and she couldn't match Lonen's physical strength.

Fortunately, she'd managed to persuade him that they needed the magical artifact and he'd agreed to bring it with them. She'd know how to handle it better next time.

There had to be a next time.

She didn't know what extremes she might've gone to if he'd insisted on leaving it behind. Or worse, if he'd walled it up again in that tomb behind stones too heavy for her to budge. Though, if he had gone to such an extreme, she could perhaps have used magic to change the balance of power between them.

She'd barely begun to practice magic in active ways before they fled Bára. Leaving her home—and the deep, ancestral well of sgath magic beneath the walled city—had stripped her of her birthright of power along with her crown. Now the short and overwhelming session with the mask had filled her with such immense reservoirs of sgath magic that she bubbled over with it. She had little experience, and no doubt even less dexterity, at converting passive sgath to active grien to use it as a tool, but she possessed plenty of punch.

Enough to overcome Lonen. Just to take the mask. That's all.

The unfamiliar power tingled in her fingertips, begging to be released, to be exploited…

TITLES BY JEFFE KENNEDY

FANTASY ROMANCES

BONDS OF MAGIC
Dark Wizard
Bright Familiar
Grey Magic
Familiar Winter Magic (In Fire of the Frost)

HEIRS OF MAGIC
The Long Night of the Crystalline Moon
(also available in *Under a Winter Sky*)
The Golden Gryphon and the Bear Prince
The Sorceress Queen and the Pirate Rogue
The Dragon's Daughter and the Winter Mage
The Storm Princess and the Raven King (May 2022)

THE FORGOTTEN EMPIRES
The Orchid Throne
The Fiery Crown
The Promised Queen

THE TWELVE KINGDOMS
Negotiation

The Mark of the Tala
The Tears of the Rose
The Talon of the Hawk
Heart's Blood
The Crown of the Queen

THE UNCHARTED REALMS
The Pages of the Mind
The Edge of the Blade
The Snows of Windroven
The Shift of the Tide
The Arrows of the Heart
The Dragons of Summer
The Fate of the Tala
The Lost Princess Returns

THE CHRONICLES OF DASNARIA
Prisoner of the Crown
Exile of the Seas
Warrior of the World

SORCEROUS MOONS
Lonen's War
Oria's Gambit
The Tides of Bára
The Forests of Dru
Oria's Enchantment
Lonen's Reign

A COVENANT OF THORNS
Rogue's Pawn
Rogue's Possession
Rogue's Paradise

CONTEMPORARY ROMANCES

Shooting Star

MISSED CONNECTIONS
Last Dance
With a Prince
Since Last Christmas

CONTEMPORARY EROTIC ROMANCES

Exact Warm Unholy
The Devil's Doorbell

FACETS OF PASSION
Sapphire
Platinum
Ruby
Five Golden Rings

FALLING UNDER
Going Under
Under His Touch
Under Contract

EROTIC PARANORMAL

MASTER OF THE OPERA E-SERIAL
Master of the Opera, Act 1: Passionate Overture
Master of the Opera, Act 2: Ghost Aria
Master of the Opera, Act 3: Phantom Serenade
Master of the Opera, Act 4: Dark Interlude
Master of the Opera, Act 5: A Haunting Duet
Master of the Opera, Act 6: Crescendo
Master of the Opera

BLOOD CURRENCY
Blood Currency

<u>BDSM FAIRYTALE ROMANCE</u>
Petals and Thorns

Thank you for reading!

About Jeffe Kennedy

Jeffe Kennedy is a multi-award-winning and best-selling author of romantic fantasy. She is the current President of the Science Fiction and Fantasy Writers of America (SFWA) and is a member of Romance Writers of America (RWA), and Novelists, Inc. (NINC). She is best known for her RITA® Award-winning novel, *The Pages of the Mind*, the recent trilogy, *The Forgotten Empires*, and the wildly popular, *Dark Wizard*. Jeffe lives in Santa Fe, New Mexico.

Jeffe can be found online at her website: JeffeKennedy.com, on her podcast First Cup of Coffee, every Sunday at the popular SFF Seven blog, on Facebook, on Goodreads, on BookBub, and pretty much constantly on Twitter @jeffekennedy. She is represented by Sarah Younger of Nancy Yost Literary Agency.

jeffekennedy.com

facebook.com/Author.Jeffe.Kennedy

twitter.com/jeffekennedy

goodreads.com/author/show/1014374.Jeffe_Kennedy

bookbub.com/profile/jeffe-kennedy

Sign up for her newsletter here.

jeffekennedy.com/sign-up-for-my-newsletter